IN HOT WATER

IN HOT WATER

❀

Meg Capri

iUniverse, Inc.
New York Lincoln Shanghai

In Hot Water

iUniverse, Inc.

For information address:
iUniverse, Inc.
2021 Pine Lake Road, Suite 100
Lincoln, NE 68512
www.iuniverse.com

This is a work of fiction. Any resemblance to persons, places, or entities is purely coincidental and not intended by the author.

Music lyrics from *Same Old Ways*, copyright Sharon Dahm, all rights reserved, used with permission by the artist.

ISBN: 0-595-31179-2

Printed in the United States of America

To the usual suspects:

Bill for listening
Sharon for musing
Ruth for reading
Sheryl for laughing

…and Wuff for drinking Green Monkey Tea

CHAPTER 1

❀

All my life I've loved tea. That's no exaggeration—for as long as I can remember, tea has brought me either strength or solace, eased me through bouts of PMS or the flu or hangovers, even cleared up puffy eyes. (Use two chilled bags of Orange Pekoe as a compress for ten minutes, then rinse with tepid water.) One of my earliest memories is being about four or five and drinking from my grandmother's china teacups with the pattern of violets and faded gilt rims; she would brew a pot of Constant Comment and take hers straight, then add three-quarter's worth of milk and sugar to mine. We would also make cucumber sandwiches and batter biscuits and eat the biscuits while they were still steaming with gobs of butter and strawberry jam. At that time my mother was in full free spirit mode and very unreliable so Gran meant everything to me, and tea seemed the magic potion that kept us together. That kept me close to my grandmother's gentle voice and nice, clean yellow house with the porch swing and the lilacs, to her quiet rooms with the clocks ticking and cats padding here and there—as opposed to life with my mother, which was one strange babysitter after another, paints and canvases all over, graham crackers and Velveeta for dinner, boyfriends that varied with the season if they even lasted that long, and my mother herself, who was fond of walking around naked or painting naked while blasting Joni Mitchell and who often forgot to wake us up to go to school.

But I cleared up issues with my mother long ago; there's no lingering resentment. Well, not usually. We just could never live under the same roof again—not that we really had a roof through most of my childhood, because Mother had knocked out a considerable portion of it so that she could work on a series of portraits called Cryptic Cosmic Sky and Stars.

Anyhow, so now I'm just thirty and run a tearoom in a Chicago neighborhood called Ravenswood, which is a pretty staid place. Mostly older courtyard buildings, Victorians with wide lawns, ethnic restaurants, antique shops. No mod galleries; none of the hip clubs of Wicker Park or the boutiques of Bucktown. About the quirkiest thing going on in Ravenswood is the occasional sight of someone carrying a mandolin or banjo over to the Old Town School of Folk Music for a lesson. I like Ravenswood because I'm a freak about being calm and centered. Having grown up in such a wiggy manner, I like quiet; I like living on a block with buildings that have been there for over a century; I don't need the urban thrill of gang graffiti, martini ranches or stoop parties. I like my big glass canisters of Darjeeling and Assam and my brown and white sugar cubes, my steam kettles and the soft oak wood tones of my tearoom. Though I did opt for beaded lampshades and red velvet curtains in the décor and my teacups deliberately don't match—they're odd ones I've collected over time. And I can read tea leaves and enjoy fooling around with Tarot cards, which means maybe I've got some of my mother's quirky gypsy soul in me too, but I'd say it's more the pragmatic gypsy type. The gypsies who can set up camp in the middle of nowhere, drape fabric here and there, light a few sticks of incense and create an illusion of other exotic worlds.

My hair and eyes are dark like a gypsy too, though I have paper-pale skin. This is because Mother spent the winter before I was born in Spain and Portugal. For years I only knew my father as some Spanish or Portuguese guy my mother got involved with, but since it could have been one of six she never pursued actualities. Not knowing who your father is can make you a freak about being calm and centered too. But I never really wanted to meet him or have any teary airport reunions; I only wanted to confirm a certain image I'd always had of this man who gave up a few jets of himself to bring me to life: he would be dark, he would be handsome, with full lips and magnetic eyes; he would strum a guitar and watch the blonde braless heedlessness of my mother with fascination, yet then shake his head, mouth the word *loca*, and pause to take a sip of good hot tea.

When I first started the tearoom, which I called Samovar, I wasn't in hot water. I was in perfect water, like the temperature of a bath when it's just right, not too warm or cold, as easy and blissful as being back to floating in the womb. I was engaged to David, who I was truly and comfortably in love with and who for a long time I'd considered to be my soul mate. That's a sappy word but to be with David was effortless—he made you laugh, he made you feel desirable, he remembered birthdays and occasions and bought flowers for no reason sometimes, never wanted too much or too little sex—yet he also managed to keep a bit of an edge and male mystique, a few fun cards up his sleeve so that you weren't bored, although maybe there was one too big hidden screaming Joker behind the cuff, as I would find out later on.

At the time, however, we were fine, informally engaged though somewhat stalling on marriage and planning for a wedding within the next two years. David was the child of a nasty divorce and I was the child of a boho painter and one unknown Latin, so perhaps each of us had our reasons to be skeptical about conjugal bliss. But we were always together, beyond David's work as a patent attorney and my time at the tearoom; we had met at a dinner party of some mutual friends following college, and I remember when I had sat next to David at the table with the floating candles in the shape of lotus petals and potato-leek soup I had felt like I was a jigsaw puzzle piece fitting neatly into place. He curved outward where I curved inward; he was yang, I was yin; he was the sun, I was the moon; we were always in balance. His body was broad and well-muscled and I liked the solidity to it along with his strong features and wide gray eyes. I even liked his wire-rimmed glasses and how he had three pairs of them that he was always misplacing. There was never any tension or confusion as to the definition of our relationship: we moved from that dinner party to a few official dates, then to regular weekends, and then we were somehow living together and talking about next year when we go on vacation or honey have you seen my toothbrush.

"He makes you feel safe," my mother noted. "You crave that…you always have."

"Gosh, I wonder why," I replied, rolling my eyes and mouthing the word *loca*, though I didn't have a guitar handy and we were drinking iced hibiscus tea because my mother shunned caffeine.

"He has some deep passions though," she speculated. "You should try to tap into them. I'll bet he's good in bed. Nice and lusty."

David was methodically lusty but I wasn't about to tell her that or get any lovemaking tips or positions from the *Kama Sutra*. I also didn't want to discuss passion with my mother because she was always accusing me of trying to control life and avoid excitement, not noting the connection that it was her passion and lack of control that had skewed me back that way. So that I now found passion disruptive and disturbing and like too much hot water. It caused sweat and discomfort; it could scorch and scald you. Of course you can't make good tea unless the water is boiling hot, but then in the tea-making process the hot water is controlled by the tea maker—something I found to be of great importance. It's not that I disliked passion; I just wanted to be sure I could control it, which my mother felt was contrary to the very nature of intensity and desire. But then I thought my mother was irresponsible and had round heels.

"It will hit you someday, Liz," my mother further advised, shaking back her still mostly blonde flowing mane. "It will pull you out of yourself and you'll never be the same."

Blah blah, yeah yeah, I would always think. Come get me and rock my world. By the way, my name is Liz because it's short for Alizarin. That's a deep red pigment used in painting. We're all named for pigments and tones—I'm Alizarin, my brother is Orpiment and my sister is Umbra. Those are our crazy names given to us by our mother; we also have street names for the real world, like I took on Liz, Orpiment settled for Pete, and Umbra became Amy. Amy's father is Scottish and unknown (mid-seventies Glasgow trip), and Pete was anonymously conceived in either San Francisco or Toronto so that he could become literally one of the first babies of the eighties (January 1 at 12:06 a.m.), though Pete has expressed a clear preference for being Canadian since he drinks Molson and plays hockey very well.

Pete also designs websites and comes into Samovar almost every day, but Amy has left us and married a holy roller, *i.e.,* a Baptist from southern Indiana. She was wooed away by the pairs of them who used to spread the word in our neighborhood and hand out small pamphlets that asked **ARE YOU HEADED FOR HELL?** Amy was always an interesting combination of demure and sex-starved, and she was primarily fond of clean-cut boys in suits so she was easy Baptist fodder. She was looking for direction and focus and a steady male influence. If the Baptists hadn't gotten to her first she probably would have ended up in a cult, and as it is now she's cut nearly all ties with her past, though she did just send me a nice crocheted tea cozy in the shape of a lumpy cottage, along with several pamphlets about my being headed for hell in both Spanish and English.

I started to slip into hot water when I first met the Catapano brothers, Joe and Mike. In fact, they were the hot water or at least the flames that began to make things boil. They ran a place at the end of the block called the Caffè Napoli that served sandwiches and pastries and hot chocolate, coffee and espresso. The Napoli and Samovar were never in competition, since we each offered a different ambience and I never sold substantial food like they did, just scones and tarts and brioche, but we were on the same block of Wilson Avenue by the El tracks and Mike was initially territorial. Mike was the elder brother by a few years and Joe was about my age. Before I had opened officially and was painting the walls of the tearoom and hanging curtains and all, I stopped by the Caffè Napoli for something to eat and introduced myself to Joe, who I liked right off because he reminded me of David. He was handsome and bespectacled, and he had the same compact build and wry humor. He also made incredible hot cocoa, with real hot milk and chocolate squares topped by a cloud of whipped cream and cinnamon. His minestrone was awesome and his provolone and roast beef sandwich had just the right amount of dressing, just the right amount of red pepper, just the right everything.

Joe was a genius behind that green marble counter, while his brother handled the more business-like details such as finances, advertising, and inventory. When I first met Joe, Mike was engaged in a heated finger-pointing argument with the guy who delivered bread and I didn't wait to see the outcome. Mike then followed me back to the tearoom and came in when I was starting to paint again, nearly scaring me into falling off the ladder and telling me that I shouldn't leave front doors open.

"What if a crazy person wandered in and killed you," he said. "You're in Chicago, it's a crime capital. Be careful."

It was a hundred degrees that day and I of course had no air conditioning installed yet; I only had an oscillating fan on the floor that was basically creating a mini-vortex of heat and paint fumes. By the time Mike barged in I was starting to feel woozy from the bad combo of Dutch Boy Coral Reef and an enclosed, hot space. I felt myself teetering on the ladder slightly and looked at him in confusion.

"You were talking to my brother before," he prompted. "Down the street. We run the Caffè Napoli. He's Joe, I'm Mike. And you're Liz, right?"

"Yes," I said, stepping down and trying to get my bearings. Mike was tall, dark, hard-bodied, with a sharp nose and a scar going from his lower lip across his chin, like somebody had punched him with brass knuckles once upon a time. The scar was barely noticeable but if you looked closely you could see it, like a pale crooked seam. While I stood unsteadily studying him and the scar I kept hearing the theme from *Charles in Charge* in the back of my head, and then I realized that he reminded me of a bigger, more arrogant version of Scott Baio. Like if Scott had gone to prison and pumped iron and been hit in the face with a chain, maybe. I smiled, thinking of this.

"What's funny?" he asked. He was looking me up and down as well; he was the type who visibly looked you up and down, measuring, gauging, envisioning, straddling. "You seem dazed," he noted. "You should take a break, this place is a sweatbox. Here, I brought you something."

To his credit he had an Orangina and a cup of ice in a paper bag, along with a three-nut brownie. I knew they were three-nut because the Caffè Napoli was famous for them: walnut, almond, and pecan amid swirls of dense moist black sweetness.

"This is how I get my energy to spike," he explained. "Orange juice and chocolate. It's a quick fix but it works. Come on," he urged. "Let's go sit in the alley and talk…it's cooler there."

I think I would have followed him off a bridge to get that Orangina and brownie, so we went and sat on the stoop outside the shop's back door and I ate and drank while Mike watched.

"You look pale," he observed.

I nodded, chewing. "I always do. Even when I feel great."

"Yeah, you've got that china doll skin thing," he said. "It's very pretty."

He had an offbeat, casual tone but I flushed deeply when he made that comment, and for a moment I could feel a charge of energy between his arm and my own as we sat side by side. His arm was strong and brown with a thick sinew like a rope running through it. His eyes were half-lidded and still assessing me and seemed as dark and lethal as the brownie I had just finished. *Turn away*, I thought. *You can't handle this type of person and you don't want to even try.*

Mike appeared not be feeling the same charge between us and instead was talking about himself and his brother and how they were originally from Chicago Heights, a suburb where Al Capone used to sell a little hootch; how he liked small business owners and the whole spirit of entrepreneurship; how he had rented the apartment above the Caffè Napoli, knocked down the walls and turned it into a big open space with skylights and a rooftop garden.

"I don't think we'll be in too much competition," he concluded. "To be honest, I'm glad you're here. You should have seen what was in this storefront before, some nasty old crank selling crap like lice combs and Fresca. All the Fresca cans were rusty and about ready to explode and there was a dead mouse by the register for about a year. But it looks like you'll have a nice place. Welcome."

He smiled warmly while I stared back in a daze again, not because of the heat but that smile was so charming. He could look mean but he could also look incredibly caring and tender. That's because he's like Satan, I thought. Satan who is totally unfazed by heat and humidity and the fact that the new pavement they had put in the alley last week had begun to melt and buckle and steam.

"It's a hundred and three now," Mike said, also diabolically reading into my thoughts. "I love this weather, I was made for the tropics. Come stop by and say hi," he insisted, getting up to leave. "If you don't see me there with Joe, I'm usually in the backroom or up in my place. I use that as an office too. Good to meet you, Liz. Take care."

He paused, shook my hand once more and helped me to my feet. "Speaking of heat, I just remembered something my Dad used to tell us," he said, laughing. "He'd get a bad cold every winter and drink tea instead of coffee. And he'd always comment that people and teabags were the same, because you never knew how much they had in them until you put them in hot water. You believe that?"

"It makes some sense," I said. I vaguely recalled hearing that before, that it had been a comment made by Eleanor Roosevelt or Nancy Reagan. One of those controversial hot water-type First Ladies.

"You're married?" he asked, glancing at my hand. David had given me a pearl and ruby antique ring for Valentine's Day; it had originally been his great-grandmother's and had served three generations of fiancés.

"Engaged," I replied.

"Can I see?" He reached for my hand again and examined the ring. His fingers were long and calloused and I could feel either his pulse or my own beating between our layers of skin. "Pretty. I'd get you an opal, though," he added. "You kind of remind me of an opal yourself, maybe. Pale but with fire inside."

I drew my hand back, startled. The opal is my birthstone and favorite of all, because it's so iridescent and unique. Mike waved and moved on.

"What *guy* knows about opals…he is the Devil," I murmured, and though I didn't want to I watched him walk with a bit of a swagger down the alley, like he knew I was watching and wanted to give me a good show.

CHAPTER 2

❦

A few weeks after that initial meeting, I opened Samovar for business and hired two waitresses. I tended to hire a certain type who would lure in male customers, which was calculating of me but it also seemed to work. I was looking for hip and friendly and/or hip and ethereal, but I didn't want tragically hip or hostile—that was a definite no-no. My goal was to create a pleasant funky setting where anyone from eighteen to eighty would feel at ease. I wanted the older ladies who liked to dawdle over tea and think about exotic places they had never been to; I wanted the commuters who needed to rush in and grab something quick but different from the usual donut and coffee; I wanted the Greek neighborhood men who would sit and play chess or yell about philosophy; and I wanted local artists and writers and poets to make it their "spot."

And it did become a spot, fairly quickly, and I enjoyed watching the success and seeing my investment blossom. I had my waitresses Thea and Gemma, Thea being the more assertive hipster with a belly ring, carmine-streaked hair and tales of adventures and LSD parties I'm not sure she had actually attended, but she talked a good game; while Gemma was quieter, with glass-green eyes and fairy-like features, quite seriously studying the cello whenever she wasn't working for me. Oftentimes I helped behind the counter or waited tables too, but I was generally busy with other more nuts-and-bolts things—so busy that I only saw David in the evenings. But he was always busy himself as an attorney and rarely complained, and he would stop by after his own long day to pick me up and help me close for the night.

In terms of tea personification, David was Russian. Tea personification is my habit of classifying a person as a tea, and I'm always doing it subconsciously—it's just reflexive. Like there are some people who are regular Lipton in a bag—dependable, standard, enduring—and then there are types like my sister Amy who would be peppermint, non-caffeinated, optimistic, naïve and longing to do good. (Peppermint soothes the stomach, of course.) My mother was her favorite brew, hibiscus, scarlet and fruity but lacking a certain substance; my brother Pete would have to be green tea, because he's all earthy and intense and has a hemp leaf tattooed on his palm and because he does drink green tea in vast quantities, whether iced or hot.

I'm Chai, because there's that no-nonsense base of black tea undercut with cardamom and clove, though I could be Black Peach too; but David to me was always Russian, specifically Russian Caravan. Strong but not too forceful, with a subtle undercurrent. My first boyfriend was a teaching assistant in college who chain-smoked and talked about the beauty of numbers and he was Lapsang Souchong. I can hardly even taste that smoky musky tea without thinking of him and his Dunhills and the strange numerical code in which he wrote love letters. Generally I can look at a person and within a minute or so figure out what tea they're going to ask for. Before I met David he had never had Russian tea but when I made a glass for him (you should drink Russian tea in glasses: it's so *Dr. Zhivago*) he was hooked.

One night after Samovar had been open for about six months, he came in and had his glass of Caravan like he always did each night while I counted out the register and decided which pastries could be salvaged and which would be best brought home as leftovers. David seemed tired and was getting a cold. A crazy sleeting wind lashed against the windows and buffeted the awning of my shop along with all the others up and down the block.

"Are you okay?" I asked, pausing to massage his shoulders. He took off his glasses and wiped some hot tea condensation from the lenses, then sighed.

"I don't know," he said. "I just feel…like I'm not doing what I'm supposed to. Like I'm miscast or something."

"How so?" I said, sitting down across from him. I was partly fearful yet partly fascinated, because David never talked like this—he never had soul-searching moments, or at least not any that he voiced. He had always seemed quite happy practicing law and living in Chicago and driving to his cottage in Galena that he'd bought two summers ago. He had been the one to suggest marriage and children, and I had thought that was all part of his natural inclination.

He touched my cheek. "Whatever it is, it's not you," he answered quietly. "I like this and being together, I always have. But there's something else…it's hard to explain. It's close to impossible to explain."

His face was serious. Usually David had a glint or a gleam in the eye or was ready to make a clever remark, but now his expression was confused and almost haggard.

"Do you want to end the engagement, or maybe take a break?" I asked. I thought he was talking about wanderlust or needing to sow some oats, and while at first the whole idea gave me a moment of panic, I then became calm and rational because above all David was my best friend and I wanted him to be happy. And because even though I wanted to marry my best friend and live in the nice house with the porch swing and the lilacs like my grandmother's, I didn't want there to be any doubts. I wanted all doubts gone, beaten out like lumps in cake batter.

"No," he said, with effort. "I just—"

We were interrupted by a banging on the door even though I had flipped the CLOSED sign around. But it was Mike and Joe stopping by, Mike seeming worked up and wild, like the weather.

"Someone's pretending to be a City Health inspector," he announced with contempt. "And then they find phony violations and scam you for five hundred dollars in fines. It happened to the Thai restaurant on Montrose Avenue and the pancake house on Lawrence. So be aware."

I noticed Mike sizing David up shrewdly, and then he introduced himself. Joe introduced himself as well and I smiled while watching him shake David's hand, because they almost looked like twins. I had mentioned Mike and Joe before to David and he knew who they were immediately. I saw Joe often because I liked to start my morning with one of his hot chocolates, and every once in a while he would walk over with a sandwich or some pasta salad for me, because like I mentioned, I didn't really serve any substantial lunch food. Joe was Russian tea of course, too, and Mike was probably Assam...I hadn't quite decided. But he'd be the richest darkest strongest tea possible. The type of tea that would make your mouth pucker from its force yet then leave you eager for more.

"Did Gemma go home?" Mike asked, glancing around. Mike was surprisingly keen on Gemma, surprising because I would have thought he'd prefer Thea and her free and easy demeanor. And her spider web tattoo and big boobs—Gemma like myself was unmarked and on the more delicate 34B side.

"She left with Pete. I think they might be getting involved," I said, trying to put it as gently as possible because Mike appeared smitten.

"Ouch," Joe murmured, putting his hand over his heart. "Mike's been shot...he's wounded. Mike is dead."

"I'm not dead, stupid," Mike scoffed. "It takes a lot more than that to kill me. Gemma's just nice…pretty and talented too. I saw her play the cello last week at a recital. She was great."

"You went to her *cello* recital?" I demanded. "Wow, you're determined."

"Mike walks the extra mile," Joe put in. "For the right girl. Otherwise he just walks to the corner drug store."

"To buy Trojans," Mike laughed.

"I was trying to be subtle," Joe smiled back. "Implied humor."

David regarded Joe with interest then, probably because he was realizing why Joe reminded me so much of him.

"Is your brother a flake or should I not bother trying to wait this out?" Mike persisted, picking up a quarter that I had missed as a tip off one of the tables and handing it to me.

"He can be a flake," I said. "It could end in a month or two. Or Gemma could get sick of him. That's more likely."

"I'll back off but keep circling for signs of weakness," Mike decided. "Hey, you're a lawyer, right?" he then asked, nodding at David. "Maybe you can help Joe out."

It was revealed that Joe had a girlfriend named Vivienne whom he hoped to marry, only she was currently stuck in France. Because upon coming here on her last visit, customs agents had skimmed through a journal she was keeping and seen how she had written about getting married to Joe. Which would make her a U.S. citizen, which had touched off suspicions of green card fraud, which had her indefinitely detained in her native land.

"How ridiculous," I said. "It's not like you were trying to pull a scam. You really want to get married, don't you?"

"No…I mean yes," Joe said after a moment. "It's not a scam."

"I'm not an immigration attorney but I can talk to a few at my firm," David offered, handing Joe one of his business cards. "Call me at the end of the week and I'll let you know what they suggest."

Joe thanked David and Mike advised us that the moral of the story was never to put anything in writing. The Catapano brothers then went back into the dark and stormy night and I sat down with David again. His tea had become cold but he didn't want a refill.

"We can keep talking about what we were discussing before," I offered. "I don't mind."

"I know you don't mind…that's why I love you," he said, taking a red carnation from the vase on the table and sticking it behind my ear. "You little Spanish dancer. You look like a flamenco dancer when you pull your hair back in a bun like that. Or like you should be doing the tango with that guy Mike."

"With Mike?" I laughed, somewhat intrigued by the concept. "Why not with you?"

David shrugged. "He's got the right build, the right features."

"I can't tango, though," I said.

"He'd teach you." David took a bottle of cough syrup from his briefcase and took a long swallow, grimacing. "God, that's awful. Like cherry-flavored turpentine."

"I want you to know that you can tell me stuff," I urged again, getting up to hurry and finish cleaning: it was nearly eleven o'clock and I was sure David was wiped out. "Even if you think it might upset me or our relationship."

"Yes, ma'am," David said, blowing his nose, and then he pointed to me and the broom I was carrying. "Dance the tango," he insisted. "Go on, give it a shot."

I did one campy pass, lunged and spun around. David laughed.

"You're a natural," he pronounced, putting his head on the table to take a quick nap while I packed up the leftover pastries and shut the place down for the night.

CHAPTER 3

❀

The next day my mother dropped by in super-high spirits because she had sold two paintings. She flounced in in a long turquoise dress that matched her eyes, hair streaming behind her in a disarray of silvery blonde curls and leather thong sandals flapping crisply. She had brought me a present of five yards of iridescent fabric, lovely copper crepe with purple rippling through it, while for Pete she had bought a pair of high-power military binoculars to replace the current plastic ones that he used for bird watching and/or spying on the other apartment dwellers around him. She had a glass of iced hibiscus and a slice of zucchini bread, told Pete that his eye whites were cloudy and therefore he wasn't eating enough fruit, met Gemma and discussed the cello and whether Pete was attentive to Gemma's womanly needs (*i.e.*, oral pleasure) and thereby embarrassed the two of them into a rapid departure. And then she turned to me.

"Liz, are you really getting married or is that a bust?" she asked, raising her bright glass then sucking at a lemon wedge speculatively. Her eyes were splendid in the afternoon light and I could see various people glancing at her with interest. My mother, Beth Miller, was a fairly well known model back in the late sixties and early seventies. She was on magazine covers and print ads; she partied with rock stars. She even kept in touch with a few of those rock stars during their reunion tours, and I remember coming home from the twelfth grade once to find a major legend in our kitchen buck-naked and making a cup of tea. He drank English Breakfast and covered himself with a potholder for my benefit. I saved the tea bag for years, of course, until it crumbled into dust.

"We'll get married eventually," I said. Although David hadn't again raised the issue of what he was doing with his life and presumably what I was doing in it, he was still in a curious mood. He took forever to make decisions—even over trivial things, like what brand of toilet paper to buy—and he was sleeping a lot. He came home from work and went straight to bed, then on weekends took long naps burrowed deep under the covers. I knew that sleeping was a sign of depression, but I also thought he might just be going through a seasonal funk, as David tended to get a little down every year around the holidays. Then New Year's would pass and he would visit his mother and stepfather in New Mexico and his father and stepmother in Arizona (the Desert Classic Tour as we called it), get some sun and perk up.

"What paintings did you sell?" I asked my mother, because I wanted to change the subject and she was always gabby about her art.

"The one of the man in the steam room and the paisley tiger. That's why I'm so excited," she elaborated. "They were my *real* stuff, not those damn flowers."

Those damn flowers were what my mother made most of her money on, huge exploding poppies or roses or lilies, in the vein of Georgia O'Keeffe but not as precise and perfect. My mother painted fast because she had a short attention span, but she was intuitively skilled and could give a flower lots of passion. People tended to opt for the flowers because of their decorative appeal, whether in a home or corporate setting, and Mother's gallery agent liked to link the floral paintings with my mother's past career as Beth Miller the Model, to give an extra push to the sale. Incidentally, my mother left modeling at the top of her game because she was bored with the fatuous attention and with sitting in front of a camera. Though she did like the rockers and the money and the free clothes and jewelry and perfume she used to get. Boas, velvet halters, Pucci jackets, endless strands of amber: I remember all my friends wanting to play dress-up at our house, because my mother had such amazing things in her closet and trunks.

"How's that Caffè Napoli down the street?" my mother asked, finishing her iced hibiscus. "I'd love a good espresso."

"You don't drink caffeine," I reminded. "It causes cysts and migraines and rashes and irritability and discolored teeth. Or at least that's what you've been telling me since I even knew what caffeine was."

"It does, but every once in a while I get a craving," she said. "I lived in Rome for a year, you know that. I loved espresso so much I drank it four times a day. I also had a Vespa that I rode all over the place. I was very into speed and motion then."

"Well, go have a Roman flashback," I urged. "The café's run by two brothers…they're very nice. The one behind the counter reminds me of David."

"What about the other one? Taller, with an aquiline nose?" she queried, twisting a curl around her forefinger. I smiled. So that was why my mother had an espresso craving. She had gotten a glimpse of Mike. I smiled yet then felt a hot stinging sensation that came out of nowhere and rose up through my body.

"Are you all right?" my mother asked. I forced myself to look past her and inhaled slowly.

"I'm fine," I said, but I realized I didn't want her to touch him. I didn't want her to go anywhere near Mike—but why? Normally I didn't care who my mother associated with and just had a detached air of amusement, but now I wanted to scream, to yank at a big handful of her loopy ash blonde hair and tell her to act her age and shut her legs for once. I imagined her kissing him and Mike responding and opening her mouth with his tongue, then sliding his hands down to the curve of her ass. My mother still had a good curvy ass and a fine body. Mike would have appreciated that along with her years of sexual experience. Mike would surely go for a fun fling with a famous ex-model.

I had a bone china cup in my hand and it was about to shatter. I excused myself and mumbled something about a leaking refrigerator, then went to the back and ran cool water over my wrists and splashed more water on my face. I took a deep breath and tried not to think of my mother strolling over there, walking up to Mike, smiling at Mike, who would pause from whatever he was doing and look her over, then smile back. The heat was surging up again, like mercury in a broken thermometer. Yet then I turned and saw my mother standing by my side, her blue-green eyes wide and curious.

"Are you involved?" she asked, watching closely. "With that fellow I mentioned. I've never seen you look like that. In fact," she speculated. "I think I know who your father is…Gilberto Something. When you got angry before I saw a resemblance that's never been there in the past."

"Thanks," I said curtly, drying my hands. "Now if I just search Portugal and Spain for men named Gilberto Something, I can solve this eternal mystery. And no, I'm not involved with Mike and I wasn't angry. It's just that, well, he's kind of arrogant," I found myself adding. "And a chauvinist. He doesn't like independent or assertive women. He liked Gemma," I elaborated. "Because she's sweet and quiet. I don't know that you and he would be much of a match. He'd disapprove of your entire lifestyle."

Listen to me, I thought, I am lying like some rotten catty female—and to my own *mother*, who had raised me to never be rotten or catty. I could hardly look at her for a moment. Finally, she nodded and sighed.

"Maybe you're right," she said. "You know how I hate hassles, especially with men. I don't need some guy hounding me about my ethics or my ways, or calling me too old."

"You're not too old," I insisted apologetically. "You look fantastic."

"Sure, but those types of guys are only out for DYD's," she said. "Dumb, Young, and Do What I Tell You. They can't think beyond a certain mindset. No espresso for me today," she concluded, giving me a kiss on the cheek and leaving in a gold and turquoise swirl.

I remained in the kitchen area, staring at a clump of tealeaves in the sink. I felt ashamed and stupid and petty—and confused—because what was all this heat and steam about? I didn't want to have anything to do with Mike; I was engaged to David and right now in looking down at the pattern of tealeaves I saw a happy marriage predicted and of course that would be with him. Mike was a foolish physical attraction that would burn itself up within a week. I didn't have physical attractions often so I just wasn't sure how to handle them, but when I was acting normally again and the lava had left my brain I would make a point of introducing Mike to my mother and they could French each other right in front of me for all I cared. Because I was sure that Mike could really French kiss, penetrate and probe your mouth, touch his hands to the hollows of your cheeks and draw you in for more. And then more, and then you would want to tear off his shirt like Christmas wrapping paper and feel his bare chest and that incredibly hard stomach leading downward to….

Cold water had begun to seep through the soles of my shoes and I was almost glad to see that the refrigerator was still leaking, that the mess needed to be sopped up and dealt with and I would have to stop thinking about fluttering tongues and strong, long-fingered hands—for a little while, at least.

That night I dreamt that I was in a dance contest with lots of people buzzing here and there in sequin and satin costumes. I was wearing an incredible rose chiffon dress, backless and slit to the navel, and I had my hair in a low bun with a camellia at the base and my mouth was caked with lipstick. I had no idea what I was supposed to be doing but let myself be guided along to a stage area, where I saw Mike in a white shirt and black pants. His hair was slicked back and he smelled incredible, like citrus and musk, and I found myself rushing toward him asking if we were going to tango. I was very excited and could hardly keep my hands off his body. He said that if I wanted to do that dance he would be my partner, but he wanted me to be sure of what I was getting into.

"Of course I want to dance," I insisted, pulling him toward me. "We're supposed to…David said so."

We started, legs and hips moving in perfect rhythm. I touched his back and he opened my mouth and let his tongue slip in, then we turned and went in the opposite direction and I felt all warm and like I was going to laugh and scream at the same time. Because I realized that we were somehow having *sex* while we danced; that he had gotten inside me and there was no way in hell I was going to stop him.

"You said it was all right," he kept murmuring, while I just nodded.

"Go faster…now slower…now faster," I begged. "Please."

"Anything you want," he said. "This is your show."

There was so much steam in the air and he was beautifully hot to the touch, his eyes dark and liquid. I dug my nails into his sides and watched him smile. When I woke I was digging my nails into the mattress like a crazy person.

"Oh my *God*," I whispered, immediately jolting up and turning on both bedside lamps. David was not there; he was on the first lag of his annual desert tour visiting his mother in Taos. "This is wrong," I went on to myself. "Really, really wrong. Maybe I need to see a therapist. Or an exorcist."

For some reason I felt it necessary to keep low to the ground and crawl to the kitchen, like perhaps Mike was outside watching from the street in a police surveillance van and had bugged not only the apartment but all my dreams and thoughts. I could still feel his body and the motion of his hips. I needed some chamomile tea immediately.

It was three-thirty a.m. I made the tea and put in lots of milk and sugar, then turned on the t.v. as a distraction. At that hour there were only *Andy Griffith Show* re-runs and infomercials, so I settled for Andy, Barney, Opie and Aunt Bea. Very non-sexual, calm, black and white and soothing. I drifted back to a quieter sleep, although I was lying at a strange angle on the couch and my neck was wrenched like a bent pipe cleaner when I woke. The phone was ringing and it was just sunrise. When I answered I heard a vaguely familiar male voice speaking in a strained, nervous manner.

"Liz, I need to talk to you about David," the person said.

"What?" I asked, a little groggy. "What is it?"

I was afraid there'd been an accident or something terrible had happened, and here I was dreaming about another man. But the line went dead and the phone did not ring again, and when I tried *69 to find out what the last incoming number had been the recording said that information was unavailable, and that the caller did not wish to be known.

CHAPTER 4

❀

I took a shower after the call and got dressed, still in a confused haze and caught up in the pulse and feel of that dream. I tried to avoid Mike and made a point of walking on the opposite side of the street so as not to pass the Napoli, but of course he came barging into the tearoom as soon as the morning rush had passed. I had been busy serving everyone myself, since Thea was missing in action and Gemma only worked afternoons. I took a break once the customers had dwindled to a girl studying for the LSATs and Crazy Mary, an old lady with violet hair and violet lips who wore several mangy fur stoles at a time—and I mean the kind of fur stole with the mink's beady-eyed head still attached and a clasp made out of the mouth—and that was when Mike came in. When I saw him I involuntarily lunged out of my chair, either to jump his bones or run away, I couldn't tell which urge was stronger. He saw me jolt and laughed.

"What's with you?" he said, waving to Crazy Mary, who alternated between his place and mine every other day. "It's all that tea you're drinking. It'll make you a nervous wreck. Speaking of nervous wrecks, my brother Joe's been in a bad way lately," he continued, taking a chair next to me and sampling one of the lemon tarts on my plate. "Could you ask your buddy about what's happening with Vivienne? You know, that girl in France Joe wants to marry? Only she's got major immigration problems."

"My *buddy*?" I repeated, being unnecessarily defensive. "Do you mean David, my fiancé?"

"Sure, whatever," Mike shrugged, looking at me straight on and with a slightly knowing smile. He can tell, I thought. He sees my face flushing, he can somehow feel the heat inside my body; he's like a detective of his own sexual magnetism. Although he had lemon tart crumbs on his lower lip, which wasn't too sexual or magnetic, but that lip was so full and he had a day's growth of black beard shadowing his chin and what was with those incredible eyes? I deliberately dropped my fork and upon retrieving it stuck it into the upper part of my thigh, so as to puncture any further inflation of the lust bubble.

"I don't mind asking David," I said briskly. "He's such a wonderful person. He's always helping people with legal problems. *Pro bono*. That means without charge." I was desperate; I had to fill up dead air with anything I could to keep Mike from looking so closely at me again.

"Yeah, I'm aware of the phrase *pro bono* even though I don't have a law degree myself," Mike retorted. "But David sounds like a decent guy," he added. "And it is nice of him to help Joe. I just wanted to check on the situation because like I said, Joe's really wound tight. I think he misses his girlfriend and won't take a trip there because he feels bad about leaving me alone at the Napoli. You know how it goes…small businesses are a big commitment. Do you think if I bought him a ticket and threw him on the plane he'd go? I mean, it wouldn't be easy but I'd manage. He's allowed to take a vacation."

I smiled despite the tension. I actually wanted to give Mike a hug then, mostly because of his concern for Joe and only partly because he had on an olive sweater that looked like cashmere and I wanted to find out how it and his shoulders felt.

"You're a good brother," I said, and I settled for patting his hand, but it still felt as good as cashmere and I had trouble taking my own hand away. He glanced down at my fingers.

"What's that?" he asked, noting a healed-over blister on my knuckle. "A burn?"

He touched the blister and I drew back quickly in defense. "It's from the big steam kettle," I murmured. "I get them all the time."

"Occupational hazard, I guess. But you should be more careful. Man, your skin is pretty. I think I said that before but what's the word that fits for it? Probably alabaster." He stood up and took out his wallet, then slipped me a ten-dollar bill.

"For her," he said, nodding to Crazy Mary. "Tell her it's my treat. You know, a little *pro bono* action of my own."

The ten dollars and the whole visit began to depress me suddenly, because now I knew for sure that I felt more for Mike than lust, that he had depth and humanity and heart. That he was someone you might fall in *love* with, not just want to climb on top of and ride until you could no longer walk. Unless he was conning me now—I could always hope for that.

He called over a goodbye to Mary and she raised her cup of White Pekoe in response. I watched him leave, his breath turning to frost as soon as he stepped outside, and then I watched old Crazy Mary for a moment and wished I could be her age, with all the years of emotional confusion and hormones behind me and just memories and my ratty mink wraps to keep me warm.

David returned from Taos that evening with a tan, some *paklava* from his mother (Armenian baklava), and a seemingly new purpose in life. He was full of energy and enthusiasm and picked me up and swung me around when I came through the door. He had put several vases of roses throughout the apartment—yellow in the living room, white in the kitchen, coral in the bedroom—made *coq au vin* and opened another bottle of Malesan '98 for us to finish off. I was exhausted but so glad to see him in better spirits and to just sit and be waited on myself for a change. He served me my chicken in wine sauce and marinated artichoke salad and told me to relax and enjoy the meal. I wanted to mention the anonymous dawn phone call I'd gotten, but wondered if it might have been a prank. David worked with another attorney who was overly fond of practical jokes and who had once arranged for David to take the sworn statement of a cocker spaniel. He seemed due for another charade.

"I think I got a call from John J. McFadden, Esquire this morning," I warned. "He was pretending he had something to tell me about you." I drained my glass. "Some terrible *secret*. So watch out."

David seemed uncharacteristically angry for a moment, yet then his good nature returned and he refilled my Bordeaux.

"He's a goofball," he sighed. "He never quite got the frat boy thing out of his system. I say ignore it."

Afterwards David gave me a massage with a Midnight Enchantment balm he had bought from a vendor in Taos (it smelled like rum and orange blossoms and had a swooning señorita on the label), and then he followed through with some pretty impressive lovemaking. Again I really had to do nothing but lie back and take it all in, and I was just drifting into a boozy, orangey coma of bliss when he tapped me on the cheekbone.

"Liz?" he said quietly. "Listen…I think we should elope. Forget the planning and the parents and the expense of a wedding. We'll have a party or something afterwards but for now let's just go for it. How about Valentine's Day? I know it's corny but what the hell. Okay?"

It seemed like I'd been drugged and it took me forever to focus and get my eyes open. I thought of Valentine's Day and how it was less than a month away, and how sudden it was to be confronted with something we'd been hedging around for years, but then I felt David's body against mine and the solidity of it and saw the golden brown color of his skin in the lamplight and thought how right he had felt the first time I had been with him and how he still felt so right now.

"Sure," I whispered. "That sounds fine. We'll do it."

He squeezed my hand and adjusted the sheets around us both.

"Don't tell anyone," he urged. "Not your mother, not your brother, not Gemma or Thea or whoever. It should be a total secret."

"I won't tell," I said, reaching around him to turn off the lamp and noting how his skin reminded me of toasted almonds, and how I had to order almond scones for the tearoom first thing in the morning.

"It's the right thing to do," he added in the darkness, with a curious conviction.

"Don't do it because it's right," I insisted. "Do it because you want to."

"I want to. I really, really do," he said with that same stridency, and then he held me tight until I fell back to sleep again.

And so we got ready to be secretly married, in the midst of a whirling dervish of February snow. The plan was to go to the county courthouse by David's cabin in Galena, have the ceremony there, then burrow in for a romantic weekend in the wilderness as newlyweds. We would take a honeymoon later, we decided, maybe in Portugal and Spain. This was David's suggestion, since my father was possibly Portuguese or Spanish and he thought the country might rouse something native in me, but I looked at some brochure photos of Lisbon and felt nothing. And as far as Spain was concerned while I did like flan and tapas, I certainly couldn't stand being in any country that sticks spears into bulls' necks for sport. I was hoping to sway David subversively over to London somehow—I had been to London once for only a week and loved it. So much tea, so little time.

David was now very keyed up about the marriage thing. To me, however, it was more strange than exciting, because he seemed to be acting like it was a brief to be prepared for rather than a union of souls. He was suddenly drilling me on how many children I wanted to have and what would their names be; when did we want to have these children; did we want a dog, cat, both or neither; where were we going to buy a house; did we want patterned china or gold-rimmed; did we want to combine bank accounts or maintain separate finances; and what plans did we have for our parents as they aged—would they live in a home or with us? All viable questions, of course, but for some reason I sensed that they were like facts he was gathering to build a case, but the person he really needed to convince was himself.

I kept going along with it all, nevertheless. It was time to cross that line and he was my partner, I had decided that years ago. I avoided passing by or stopping into the Caffè Napoli, and fortunately Mike was preoccupied with building a wheelchair ramp and other renovations to their place and didn't have time for me either. I was literally to the point of packing my suitcase on the morning of February 14th, slipping in something old (vintage sepia silk dress from a thrift store that buttoned up the back and fit like a glove), something new (tan suede buckle pumps), something borrowed (amber necklace from my mother), and something blue (garter belt and camisole) when my brother Pete stopped by, banging on the door like a lunatic. I had left Samovar in the hands of Gemma for the weekend and thought at first that she was having a management crisis, but he shook his head when I asked him and could barely calm himself down enough to speak.

"They called for you at the tearoom," he finally said. He was ashen and winded, like he'd been running for his life. "They thought you'd be there. Mom had a heart attack. She was taking out the trash and collapsed. She's in intensive care at Northwestern."

"What are you talking about?" I demanded, practically yelling. "A *heart* attack?! She's only fifty-seven and never eats meat. She can't possibly have had a heart attack."

"Look, that's what they told me…I'm not making it up!" he yelled back and I could see beads of sweat on his face and could feel the same cold wetness forming on the back of my neck and I knew we had to just go to the hospital and find out what was truly going on.

We drove in his piece of crap old Volkswagen Beetle that had an exhaust problem so you always had to keep the windows cracked; it was freezing and the sun soon disappeared and more snow began to fall. No one could tell us anything at the nurse's station so we went and waited outside of intensive care. Pete put his head between his legs and began to rock back and forth while I sat numbly folding and unfolding my hands, until I realized I hadn't left a note for David and he would probably come and find my half-packed suitcase and think I was a runaway bride.

I called his cell phone and said something on the voicemail, I can't remember if it made any sense, and then when I turned around a very tall doctor was standing waiting by my side. He was professional and polite, but he also had a thick accent and a loping intensity to go with the height and I couldn't focus on him as a real doctor—he looked more like a Croatian basketball player. He had numerous consonants in both his first and last names. He sat me back down in one of the waiting chairs and told me that he was terribly sorry but my mother was dead.

Dead. The word echoed and circled around my mind for several minutes, like a confused bird that had flown into a building. The word *dead* and my mother just didn't seem to fit, like the words *heart attack* and my mother made no sense. If this doctor had come to me and said your mother was killed bungee jumping or skydiving, or your mother drowned while making love with a twenty-year old waiter in Cozumel, then perhaps the concept of death would have made sense because it would have been connected with extreme life. But a heart attack—that was ridiculous.

"My mother was a vegetarian," I insisted weakly. "She ran three miles a day. She almost never drank caffeine and she stopped smoking and doing drugs twenty years ago. How could this happen?"

Dr. Kieczlovowicz closed his eyes and opened them again with resignation. I supposed it wasn't easy for him, being a kind of emissary for God, either trying to keep people alive by extraordinary measures or informing their loved ones that they had passed away. Flat-lined. Ceased to function.

"Sometimes these things are with the…um, hereditary, or hidden in the body," he struggled to explained. "And we don't know until there is no more time. And unfortunately because your mother was such healthy, there wasn't a need to find what was within. Waiting to happen…do you see?"

"Yes," I said, because in a strange way I did understand and almost appreciated his lack of technical eloquence. It made it more poignant and less medical. "My God," I whispered, feeling all energy leave me, seeping out of my veins and oozing somewhere deep into the waiting room's seashell pink carpet. I glanced over at my brother, who was almost in the fetal position.

The doctor patted my shoulder. His fingers were about six inches long. "I will come back later," he said. "For the final arrangements, but don't you should worry about it now." He nodded to Pete before leaving. "We have the grief counselors and other staff available, if you think he will have necessity for them."

I watched Dr. K. glide off like he was running for a free-throw, noting how he barely cleared the entry door back to the I.C. unit. When I broke the news to my brother he immediately snapped back *no* and started to head for the nearest exit.

"That's right, go get stoned. That's how you deal with everything," I said disgustedly. He kept walking. I supposed that I had to tell my sister Amy in Indiana but I knew her reaction would be just as aggravating—the opposite of getting stoned—probably some comment about Mom's hedonistic ways catching up with her in the long run. I felt dizzy all of a sudden thinking about my lifeless mother being wheeled down a corridor somewhere, her blonde hair still so riotously curly and streaming behind her, and I figured that I should keep moving, breathe fresh cold air, and not sit here in this creepy silent pastel waiting room. I went back through to the lobby and saw a bunch of flowers and Mylar balloons and teddy bears at the nurses' station and realized it was Valentine's Day and I was supposed to have had this as a wedding anniversary, and now it was something terrible and the holiday would always be a black one for me.

The sky beyond the glass lobby admitting doors was now violet and filled with the white swirls of a mini-blizzard. I saw David coming toward me like a shadow in his darker blue coat, and then he was holding me up because I was about to collapse, and then he had a nurse get me a wheelchair before I even knew what was happening, since I couldn't seem to walk on my own anymore.

CHAPTER 5

❀

There's so much to do when someone dies. Beyond grieving or the funeral even, beyond notifying others and scheduling a service, choosing an urn for ashes, sitting in a room full of lilies and delphiniums (even though we had asked that people just give money to Greenpeace, Mom's favorite charity) and listening to over a hundred mourners tell you how young and beautiful your mother still was…you have to do the clean-up work. My mother's services had been quite a gathering of has-beens, former lovers, ex-models, folks who'd taken one too many acid trips, and a man wearing tinted horn-rims who looked an awful lot like Warren Beatty but who disappeared as quickly as he had come.

I kept waiting for anyone who resembled the mental picture I had of my father to show up, but the closest I got was some cop named Johnny Marquez who my mother had befriended through her neighborhood watch association and who wore his gun throughout the viewing, just in case there was a riot, I supposed. A woman who had asked for several locks of Mom's glorious golden mane presented me with an amulet made from the hair and advised me that my second chakra was blocked—she had been able to feel it all the way across the room. I was the lone child in attendance, since my brother had folded after ten minutes and run home to his bong and my sister's husband had forbidden that she attend. Once everyone else had left and before they took the coffin away to prepare for cremation, I went and kissed my mother one final time and marveled at how incredible her face had been: those cheekbones, the lips, the arch of the brows. She didn't look like a corpse; she looked like a sleeping princess.

"Goodbye, Beth," I whispered. "Don't forget to write."

David was talking to the funeral director and there was a group still gathered in the reception area, ready to go party for the rest of the evening. I didn't join them but I was glad they were there, because that was what my mother had been all about, parties and laughter and being out in the world, enjoying the slideshow of life. Incidentally, there was one note that had come from the autopsy, which made me feel fractionally better about her death. Dr. K. had discovered that Mom had been taking St. John's Wort and that the herb, combined with a heated session of Bikram yoga Mom had participated in the morning of her attack, may have caused the fatal heart surge. Which didn't bring her back but if Bikram yoga and St. John's Wort had caused things, then that was more within her code of living. And dying. It was much easier to process than her death being caused by taking out the trash. Even heavy recycling would not be enough to justify that.

After the funeral I went about sorting through personal items, clothing, old photographs, bottles of shampoo, vitamin supplements, sensual oils, tax records, leases, deeds, and of course The Will itself. To my complete surprise, my mother had had a professionally prepared will and her financial affairs were in order. And she had shrewdly chosen which asset would suit which child: she had left her loft to Pete, who was a consummate city dweller and urban as a pigeon; she had left her stocks and liquid assets to Amy, because green is a color that transcends all religions; and to me she had left her artwork and any proceeds that would come of it. She had also left me her trunks full of modeling clothes and mementoes. It was surreal. I spent a week at her place alone after the services and went through everything—the boots, the boas, the photos, magazines with her heedless, perfectly chiseled aquamarine-eyed face on the cover, her creative notebooks full of sketches—and though I would be calm and focused when I started, by midnight I was usually sobbing and lying on the floor clutching a bangle bracelet or a comb still holding a few strands of her hair.

My mother had provoked and confused me for many years, I knew that, but for all our disagreements and picking at each other's moral fabric, it was somehow vital to know that I could find her in her studio blasting Fairport Convention and painting a five foot high tulip, or that she would come and find me and bring a waft of patchouli and some blue and gold light into my generally serious world. I even still expected her to come out from behind one of the wicker screens she had placed here and there to hide her painting materials, to grab me from behind and laugh and say it had all been a joke.

"Sssh, don't tell anyone," she would whisper. "I'm moving to Amsterdam…I want to make a fresh start. Just for kicks, you know? Why not."

But she never came out from behind the screens. She never came down the stairs in her yellow satin Chinese embroidered robe smeared with oil paint and she never called from the kitchenette area to tell me about the time she had eaten peyote and seen a two headed snake rise out of her own mouth. I waited and waited for her to show up, and then I began to cry. And every once in awhile I would just say her name—*Beth Miller*—aloud for no reason, maybe because I thought that in doing so I would somehow keep her alive.

I postponed the elopement for a few weeks, of course, but then I postponed it again. I couldn't explain why I was back to stalling on marriage, but felt the need to do so almost like some invisible psychic rope was pulling me gently but firmly away. I told David that I had always wanted to get married on June 21st, the summer solstice, which was true, and that I wasn't rushing into anything just to accommodate his sudden needs. Because I still swore it wasn't the burning desire to run off with me, it was more the burning desire to put up boundaries or prove something to himself. He agreed to the June plan reluctantly; I think he felt a need to hedge around me since my mother had died, that I was touchy and not quite in control of my moods.

I wasn't in control and had begun to act weird—I could see it happening but like postponing the elopement it seemed to be coming from some other force beyond me. Almost like I was possessed by my mother or part of her spirit, freaky as that may sound. I started wearing my hair loose and curly and suddenly couldn't stand the feel of a bra; I was sexually insatiable and driving David to exhaustion; I wanted to eat tons of spicy food and didn't even care for tea anymore; and one morning I found myself smudging kohl under my eyes and dabbing on blood red lipstick. Generally the only time I ever went for that color lipstick was at Christmas, when I liked to wear red velvet and the crimson seemed to fit, but suddenly I wanted to wear it now, in April. Part of me thought I looked like a slut yet part of me thought, oh, yes, this is the way to go, and for the first time in my life the *oh, yes* part was stronger, louder and clearly running the show. And to me it felt like the two headed snake my mother had bragged about in her peyote vision—something wild and frightening coming out of my mouth and I never knew what it would do next.

I had seen Mike at my mother's services and off and on since then, and he and Joe were always asking if I needed any help or just to talk—they were both quite supportive. When I started to do the sultry eyes and lips and hair thing, however, I went into the Caffè Napoli with total deliberation right before lunch hour, focusing all my attention on Mike. Mike was talking to the mailman about the White Sox's prospects and how warm the weather was; I walked past with my hair down and vampy lips and no bra beneath a sheer blouse, smiling as Mike stared and dropped all his bills and circulars. Joe didn't recognize me at first and didn't seem to care for the look, but Mike followed me to the tea-room like a tomcat in heat. I used the back entrance and still smiling slipped into our storage area and he kept following.

"Close the door," I urged, and he did. I think he was about to say how are you or what's new, but before he could form the words I had grabbed him and pressed that beautiful wide mouth against my own. And the long hard body and the hips and the measure of approval between his legs—he was so ready, I could feel it—even though he pulled away for a second to catch his breath and laugh.

"Wow," he said. "Are you drunk? Not that you should stop but I'm just curious. What kind of tea is making you act like this? You look great. Your hair and your eyes, your body…."

He pressed his lips into my throat and we kissed more, me practically swallowing his tongue; we stepped sideways around my clean-up mop and bucket; his hands went under my blouse and up toward my breasts, and then I realized what was happening and jumped back.

"Oh God, no," I whispered, my face burning—actually, I was burning all over, particularly wherever his hands had been. But now I was hot with shame, not passion. "What are you doing, Mike?!"

"What am *I* doing?" he exploded. "You come sauntering past, you lure me in here, grab me and push yourself against my zones—what the hell do you think I'm gonna do? Respond. Go for it. Grab the brass ring."

He had of course gotten my lipstick on his mouth and throat, but somehow he had also gotten kohl underneath his own eyes and I couldn't help it, it was too funny a sight. I sat down on a box of paper towels laughing hysterically, and then I began to cry.

"Christ," Mike muttered, tucking in his shirt and kneeling by my side. "What's wrong? You're still upset about your mother?"

I looked up at him almost in fear, my eyes and face wet. "I don't know," I whispered. "I think…I'm losing my mind. I have so many of these *urges*." I drifted off, staring at him; even with the smeared make-up, he was incredibly handsome. I touched the scar on his lip like I had been longing to for almost a year. He moved toward me again and opened my mouth gently with his own.

"Maybe you should follow your urges," he said, pausing for a second, and we resumed going at each other but in a slower, more sensual way and this time he was the one who stopped.

"No, I can't, I'm a schmuck," he sighed. "Your heart is beating so fast…it's like you really are drunk. It wouldn't be right." He rolled his eyes. "You're emotionally fragile or whatever the phrase is. If you did this you might go seriously crazy afterward."

"Do you think I'm going crazy?" I asked, still clinging to him.

He smiled and gave me a little slap on the cheek. "Yeah, I think you are and you're taking me with you." He eased me back toward the wall and we sat together, after Mike had readjusted himself within his pants. "Don't worry," he joked. "I give all my best advice when I have a major hard-on. At any rate," he continued. "You and I obviously have an attraction going, only I was never sure before because you had David and you kept giving me mixed signals. This was a pretty clear signal today, I'd say, like a big red arrow, but now we just need to know how to go forward. Because I don't think you're the type who wants to screw around on her fiancé. But I don't want you to leave him just for me, because what if we don't get along…that's too much pressure. And anything else that's going on is just natural, I wouldn't worry about it too much. Your mother died unexpectedly, that's a huge deal. Death always turns life inside out."

"I like you…I think you're smart and funny and physically fantastic, but really shouldn't be with you," I said, more thinking aloud than anything else. "You're a player. You don't like serious relationships and I do, and—"

"Excuse me, but how do you know what I like?" he interrupted. "Maybe I'm starting to look for serious things myself too. Especially from women who call me physically fantastic."

"Like that blonde you went to Bermuda with last month?" I shot back. "She looks real serious and stable. Like a walking blow-up doll."

"So she's a flake who wants to have fun and show off her bikini and her boob job," he said. "So what. I wouldn't get serious with *her*, no, but I'm not opposed to ever getting serious. I'm looking for quality, that's the issue. The right mind, the right values, the right sexual chemistry. And don't make any remarks about me going to Bermuda with someone—you expect me to sit around burning a candle for you while you're x-ing off days until your wedding?"

I laughed. "I can't see you burning candles for me in any way, Mike, I'm sorry. I'm just not your type."

He raised his tapered index finger and put it to my lips. "What did I tell you?" he murmured. "That you don't know everything, even though you think you do. You don't know who's whose type or what's possible. And neither do I."

"But what if I just need to get you out of my system," I wondered. "Then after I do everything will be okay again."

Mike got to his feet and dragged me up with him. "Maybe I don't want to be knocked out of your system. You ever think that? Maybe the world doesn't revolve around you and maybe I don't want to be your sex toy. Well, maybe just once or twice, and if you could wear nothing but fishnet stockings and black pumps I might be able to handle the shame."

I opened a package of paper towels and wiped the smears of make-up off his face, then he put me to rights.

"How did you get that scar?" I asked, tracing it with my fingertips again.

"From being hit in the face with a hockey stick during practice," he said. "I used to play in high school."

"Oh." I smiled. "That's not so glamorous. Or dangerous."

"See?" he noted. "You don't have it all figured out, Liz. I'm not that evil and you're not that good. Why don't you take a vacation by yourself, try to sort things out?" he suggested just before opening the storeroom door. "When I went to Bermuda it was only for a week but it was great. I know I wasn't by myself but in a way I kind of was—most of the time I tuned Brandee out and stared at the water. It's good to take a break. I keep telling my brother that but he won't listen…I guess he's waiting to have a mini-breakdown like you or just drive his car into Lake Michigan."

Mike turned to me then, however, and his eyes were dark and serious. "Sort things out and let me know what you come up with. To be honest I like David and I don't want to be the reason that you end your engagement, but I might want to be the consequence, you know?"

I nodded and watched him leave. I snuck into Samovar's little bathroom and cleaned the kohl and tear streaks off my own face, then realized like someone coming out of a dream what I was wearing. Someone get me a bra immediately, I thought—I couldn't go around showing my nips through flowered gauze like that. Although I had noticed that since I'd been opting for sheer blouses or camisoles without bras we'd had more business from a bunch of construction workers building an addition to the hospital around the corner. Suddenly they were big fans of papaya tea smoothies.

I found some band-aids in the first aid kit and put one over each breast to even things out and not have any aureoles or hard points showing through, and then I took a deep centering breath. Time to go back to business, to calm down, to perhaps sort things out as Mike had advised. Yet as I scraped the last fleck of Scarlet Temptress off my lip I remembered something that my mother had predicted about passion and how I was always dodging it: *It will hit you someday, Liz…It will pull you out of yourself and you'll never be the same.*

She had also said that she'd named me Alizarin because it was such an intense red tone and so vibrant. I'd figured she'd just had one too many pitchers of ruby-hued sangria at the time of conception and that that and some Donovan song had been her real inspiration, but maybe she had known, maybe there was something in me. And though I wasn't happy to add to the confusion I felt regarding Mike, I was secretly pleased to have sashayed past and jumped him in the storeroom. Just the look of total eager surprise had been worth it. He didn't seem like a person who was caught off-guard much and I had a sneaking suspicion that once he was, he found it pretty hard to forget.

CHAPTER 6

✿

After that I tried to channel my psycho energy into more constructive areas, like redecorating the tearoom. I used the purple and copper streaked crepe my mother had given me when she'd scored her last major painting sales and made long twisting draperies from it, then I put her artwork on all the walls. It worked well as a spring look and I got several offers on the *Peach Lily* and *Saffron Rose*, but I couldn't bring myself to sell them. They were still so much a part of her; I could just envision her slinking around before the canvases, dancing and painting and laughing. My mother had been like a painting goddess. To watch her work had been as fascinating as the works themselves.

The week before my brother and Amy and I had met with her agent and attorney for the final distribution of the will and the gallery agent chided me for not allowing any sales of her art at all, but he seemed so crass and phony that I refused to give him the satisfaction. Amy was pregnant and wearing a ruffly dress with a lace collar and white stockings, so that along with her page-boy haircut she looked like the world's largest pregnant first grader. She stuck around long enough to complain about the evils of the city, lawyers, alcohol, drugs and homosexuals, and I noticed how David shot her a hostile glance in the rearview mirror, probably because he'd heard enough evil lawyer jokes. Then we put her on a train home to glory (evidently found in Dyer, Indiana) and Pete and David and I got ready to bring Mom's ashes to his cabin. Mom had noted in her will that if possible she wanted to be given back to the earth to become part of life again, and since she had had a loft with no yard and I didn't feel comfortable sprinkling her into my houseplants, David knew a meadow that he figured would be perfect.

Pete was coming because he felt compelled to prove that he was more than an emotionally evasive slacker—to me and to Gemma, I supposed, who had broken things off because she was tired of reaching in deep yet finding no prize in the Cracker Jack box. Pete had asked Gemma to join us at the cabin but she claimed to have other plans; I felt some jealousy rising up like acid wondering if she was starting to see Mike, but when I asked her in a roundabout way she said that Mike was "too much". Which was ironic, because that was exactly what sparked me on Mike. Too much energy, too much force, too much heat pent up and waiting to be let go. Ah, the lucky woman who would be at the receiving end of that, I thought, but then I counter-reasoned that maybe it wasn't such a big deal, maybe he'd shoot off and finish in two minutes or bang you so hard that you ached and throbbed all the next day and would have to hobble around clutching a bottle of Advil with a heat-pack between your legs.

We stopped at the tearoom before we left for Galena so that I could make one final check-in with Gemma, who was again filling in for me as manager. David and Pete went to Walgreens for some last minute items but before they left Mike saw me kiss David on the forehead and watched stonily as David and Pete drove off.

"So I guess you're still the happy couple," he noted curtly. "Since I stopped you from climbing my Maypole."

"Did you?" I asked, walking right by. "I don't remember."

"You're full of shit," he said, yanking me by the arm until I shoved him away. "That's okay," he said, noting Gemma behind the counter inside the tearoom. "I'll go back to her now. Your brother screwed it up just like you predicted. She might need consoling."

"You do that," I encouraged. "And make sure you come on really strong. She likes forceful men."

I talked to Gemma for a bit then made myself an iced Chai latte, watching at first with contempt while Mike tried to hit on her once more, but then I began to feel sorry for him. She was so serenely aloof and he could never get near her—it was like watching a little boy trying to grab at a butterfly. I made him a Chai also then motioned for him to come outside.

"Yeah, what," he muttered. "She's too cool for me…what a snow queen. I think she only goes for hopheads like your brother or guys on heroin. That's her type. Half-alive, skinny, with every damn orifice pierced."

"Drink this," I urged. "It's really good."

"Why? Did you put rat poison in it or something?" he asked, but he took a sip and nodded. "It is good. Spicy. Hardly even tastes like tea."

"Never mind what she likes," I went on, smiling at his sleek dark hair and how he smelled so clean, like Irish Spring or Zest or one of those foamy virile soaps. "You're very attractive."

"I'm glad you think so as you take off with your boyfriend on a weekend lovers' trip," he scoffed. But he had appreciated the compliment, I could tell. He had a slight flush to his cheeks and his eyes were warmer and less defensive.

I explained then that we were going to bury my mother's ashes and it wasn't a total lovers' trip. Mike regarded me thoughtfully.

"You know, that's great," he said. "I think that's just what your mom would have wanted. And it's supposed to be beautiful weather too."

"But then she'll really be gone," I realized, thinking about the urn she was presently in and how I had come to focus on it and think of it as still holding an essence of my mother. When the urn was empty, there would be no immediate part of her there for me. My eyes filled with tears until Mike put his arm around my shoulders.

"No…you can't think that way, honey," he soothed. "Your mom doesn't want to be in an urn, she wants to be in the sky, flowing in the water, making more flowers like she painted. Let her go." He smiled, not in the usual cunning way but a smile that was more rare and gentle and like lifting your face to the sun. "She was a goofball hippie chick, you can't ever keep those women in one place."

"Thank you," I said, laughing and crying now. "That's a wonderful perspective."

He drained his Chai and wished me the best for the weekend. Before he left he turned to go back inside the tearoom to work on Gemma again, but then he made a face and waved his hand at her instead.

"Nah, I've got my pride," he decided. "She'll come crawling to me someday."

"If not her someone will," I promised, and then I looked in the opposite direction to watch out for David's car.

We put part of the ashes under a large chestnut tree and the other part into a stream that glinted greenish blue in the sunlight, in almost the same manner as my mother's eyes. Pete began to cry in a horrible broken-down way, and though it was painful to watch and David walked off to give him some space, I stayed and cried with him. I was only seven years older than Pete but he had always seemed like my responsibility—like a large doll for me to take care of, almost—and I had doted on him until he had started grade school and made friends of his own. We had drifted apart since then but I could still remember always making sure to take him for rides on my bike, to tuck him in at night and sometimes even sleep on the floor by the side of his bed during a period when he was having nightmares about Massive Mouse People. He had been a very open, trusting child and I supposed that time, hormones and the need to be laconic had changed him, but to feel him cry and to hold him again broke down walls that had been up for decades. I asked whether he ever regretted not having a father around.

"I don't know," he mumbled, wiping his eyes with the back of his hand. "Maybe…but not too often. Especially when I was younger, because all my friends had dads who were gung-ho about football or the army and building discipline, and I just had Mom, which was like falling through the cracks. I mean, I had Mom and you," he amended. "Because you made a huge difference. Remember Pot Roast Sundays and Lasagna Wednesdays? And how we dipped caramel apples on Halloween and decorated psychedelic Easter eggs? Those were great."

I nodded. When my grandmother had died I'd felt so dislocated and mistrustful of my mother and had pretty much offered myself up for adoption to anyone who'd take me, but once I hit my teens I came into a certain empowerment. I had found my grandmother's old cookbooks and issues of *Good Housekeeping* in the attic and decided that I was going to take her place in our multi-fathered family. So I set weekly menus and cleaning schedules and every morning would be downstairs waiting to give Pete and Amy a hot breakfast while I drank a cup of Constant Comment and finished packing bag lunches. I had made a point of celebrating holidays and starting traditions because my mother was too caught up in her own life to do it herself. Mom had been a shade condescending at first and had called me Donna Reed Jr., trying to stress that domesticity wasn't the answer to everything in life, but soon she seemed to realize that the house was running better, that I was less sullen and resentful and Amy and Pete were happier, so she actually gave me a weekly salary of forty dollars and a household account, just as long as I ensured an equal number of vegetarian dishes.

"How about you?" Pete asked now, reflectively chewing on a stem of grass. "Do you miss having a father? You know, the reason we never had them was because Mom was so independent. Not because the guys wouldn't acknowledge us or anything. Marriage or commitment gave her the willies. I'm like that sometimes," he sighed. "What if it's genetic?"

"It could be but you're also a twenty-three year old guy and that's common at your age. You just need to start *feeling* things, like you did today. It won't kill you," I said. "And maybe I do miss my father more as I get older, just because I think he is or was a lot like me. I've always had a hunch about that, but I never seem to take it anywhere so I guess it doesn't matter too much."

When we had finished talking and there was an awkward exhausted pause, David tactfully returned and brought up dinner.

"I'd say the best thing to do now is to grill as much meat as possible," he laughed. "And remember how your mother always used to scream at us about killing living creatures."

"Yeah, but I swear I caught her with barbecue sauce on her lips once," Pete said. "She was probably sneaking spare ribs and t-bones in every chance she got. Hiding stashes of beef jerky and McNuggets." A last tear rolled down into his scraggly goatee and he turned the now empty urn that had held her ashes toward him. "You goofy blonde. You're dead and Lou Reed's still crawling around. Go figure."

We went back to the cabin, where the phone was ringing and ringing. David answered heartily, still laughing, yet then he became more serious. He went into the bedroom and closed the door to talk while Pete got coals ready for the grill and I made a salad and seasoned some potatoes to roast with the meat. The food was almost done by the time David rejoined us, his face somewhat perturbed.

"Was that a client?" I asked. David generally only had conversations like that with clients, when he could bill by the hour. Otherwise he was pretty much hi and bye on the phone.

"Kind of," he said, opening a beer and drinking off half right away. "It was Joe from the Caffè Napoli. Something's going on with his girlfriend in France and he's ready to snap."

"I thought that was straightened out," I said, tossing an oven mitt to Pete, who was unsuccessfully trying to pick broiling hot potatoes wrapped in foil up off the grill with his bare hands.

"She's got problems with her documentation…the birthdates don't match," David sighed. "These things are much more complicated since 9-11, of course. Anything to do with immigration is tricky. And he doesn't really understand her and she doesn't understand him. I guess it's a language barrier but they don't seem to be communicating well."

"Mike said Joe's been pretty depressed," I noted, smoothing a cloth over the picnic table and lighting some candles. It was just dusk and still warm enough to eat outside. "Waiting for her to get here. I'm sure it's frustrating."

"He needs to get a grip," David complained, yet then he sat at the table and smiled. "This is nice, I'm glad we came," he said, raising his beer to Pete, who was approaching with a platter full of food. "A toast to the Fire King," he praised.

Pete bowed and set perfectly seared steaks, vegetable kebabs and potatoes before us.

"I do know the art of Zen grilling," he agreed, taking a beer for himself yet then pausing to uncap it and hand it to me.

"Thanks, Fire King," I said, toasting him as well, and then we all dug in like the disgusting bone-sucking carnivores that we clearly were.

The next day shortly after breakfast, I heard the crunch of tires in the cabin driveway and was surprised to see Joe of all people getting out of a car. I immediately felt a cross-wired desire of wanting Mike to be with him and absolutely not wanting Mike to be anyplace within the county line. He was alone, though, and approached us sheepishly, his head bent. He had brought some melon and prosciutto and a dozen cannoli.

"I called him back last night and told him to come up if he wanted to," David explained, taking off his glasses for a moment and blinking something out of his eye. "Because he's been such a basket case. I figured since we all like him he could hang around for a day or two. He works at that place from five a.m. to ten p.m. six days a week. He's more fried than this bacon."

David had made bacon and burned most of it. He nodded to Joe as he came in while crunching on the black crisps left in the pan. I told Joe to sit down and relax and he looked at me with such large, brown, almost shamefaced puppy eyes. The skin around his mouth was tight and I swore he had a slight tic next to his lip—I could see it pulsing away like a tiny heart.

I had planned to leave with Pete in an hour or two while David stayed through Memorial Day, but Pete was fishing out in the middle of a lake where he would probably remain until sunset or perhaps for all eternity. Although Pete preferred the city to the country, he could sit alone in absolute silence waiting forever for a fish to bite, and then as soon as he had hooked it he would throw it back into the water. He was into the Zen of fishing as much as the Zen of grilling. He had not mastered the Zen of being a guest, however, and had left wet towels all over the bathroom floor, which I went to clean up before I left. I told David that I would take the car back and he could ride home with Joe or Pete. I gathered my stuff and grabbed a cannoli for the road; David and Joe walked me to the car and David gave me an unusually long kiss goodbye.

"Drive safe, Liz," he urged. "Call as soon as you get home."

He kissed me again and glanced in at the gas gauge to make sure I had enough in the tank. I noticed how Joe watched us wistfully from the sidelines, most likely because he wanted a girlfriend to do that with as well—it seemed like Joe was a one woman man and would be very doting and affectionate, like David but maybe even more so.

CHAPTER 7

When I got back to Chicago I went straight to the tearoom, let Gemma leave and closed up early since with the holiday weekend hardly anyone was there. Mike had closed early too and was not around; I then went home and started making tentative plans for a post-elopement wedding party, just family and friends, no more than fifty people. We could have it at Samovar easily, put out a small spread and even hire a few local bands or Gemma's string quartet. If we were planning to elope on June 21, the date was coming soon and I didn't want to keep stalling on David, that didn't seem fair. I still wasn't sure whether to use a caterer or make the food myself and my head started to ache over the pros and cons of each, so I drew a nice oily sandalwood-lavender bath and slipped in with a glass of vodka-spiked chilled blackberry tea and was feeling pretty buzzed and happy after about fifteen minutes.

It had begun to rain and outside I could hear the sound of water splattering and draining from gutters and eaves onto the pavement below; it was all so soothing that I nearly fell asleep but then someone rang the front bell and I figured it was David. Once it started to rain at the cabin he tended to immediately hit the road; there wasn't much to do there when the weather was crappy. I answered the door in my robe, keeping the chain lock on just in case. Which was a good thing, because of course it wasn't David on the other side of that chain, it was Mike.

He was dripping wet yet seemed unaware that it was pouring.

"Look, I can't think straight," he said, reaching in and unhooking the chain easily, like it was a joke to even have a chain on the door in the first place. "We need to talk. I know David's in Galena, I just spoke to Joe and he said he and Pete and David are playing poker."

"Pete's going to win," I said vaguely. I still had a good vodka tea buzz on and my blood was warm and loose from the hot bath. "He acts like he's stupid and out of it but he's a shark at poker. He has a sequential theory about the cards...it' s incredibly boring to listen to but it seems to work."

Mike shrugged. "I don't care who wins, just as long as my brother's doing something different and not worrying about his girlfriend or whether we're out of eggs or the espresso machine needs cleaning. I told him, go up there and stare at a frigging cow but *just go up*. Jeez. Hey, can I have a towel?" he asked. "I was taking a walk and it started coming down like a fire hose."

He smoothed his hands back along his wet head to push out the moisture while I just stood staring. Because he now looked like he had in my dream about the tango-sex dance, his hair slick and gleaming. I went to get a towel and nearly knocked over the small oak foyer table that we put the mail on.

"I like your robe," he commented, touching the silk sleeve of it lightly. "Were you taking a bath? Do I have timing or what?"

The last of the tub water gurgled down the drain, almost as if in reply. "Mike, you really shouldn't be here," I said, but that worked about as well as the chain lock.

"Sssh, quiet, hear me out," he urged, moving me toward the bedroom while I made useless flailing gestures of protest. "I just think maybe you were right, we need to get this out of our systems. We should try to sleep together once, as a scientific experiment, because if it's terrible we'll know right off and won't waste any more time on the subject. And if it's great, then we'll know we need to do something on a bigger scale. Like end an engagement."

"I can't," I said, trying to get up but then I also let him lean in on top of me and open my robe. As he eased forward a milk crate full of old LPs that had belonged to my mother tipped over, splaying them across the rug. He was kissing me everywhere now and I had my hands in his damp hair and even though I was still saying *I can't* I was pushing my hips against him and feeling extremely overjoyed that he had opened his fly.

'You see?" he insisted, his voice becoming thick and excited. "It's for the best. We need to know. Figure it all out before anybody gets married or walks away from something they shouldn't. I love your skin, baby. Mmmm, it's so smooth and white...let me taste it, come on."

I was ready to go off from just that and the sheer pressure—he didn't even need to slip it inside—he was doing the job through his underwear, but I knew once I did that would be it. So if I was going to stop it had to be now, otherwise it would be like popping a champagne cork. Stop him, I thought. Stop. STOP.

Why weren't the words coming out? They were in my brain but weren't making it past my lips. Maybe because my lips were fused with his and again I was trying to swallow his tongue.

He went for a condom and I still didn't do a damn thing, yet then we both happened to glance at a framed picture on my nightstand and our eyes met and we froze. It was a black and white photo of David in college, taken in front of a Belmont Avenue antique store. He was standing by a statue of a winged goddess, smirking and cupping her marble breast. I had always liked the photo because of his smirk and because he had still had a punky look to him, with darker Elvis Costello glasses and long sideburns. He had become more conservative in law school but before then had hung around with a fairly offbeat crowd.

"David," I said, like he was right there with us.

Mike got up abruptly and went to the kitchen, where I heard him opening the refrigerator and rooting through drawers. He returned with a Ziploc bag full of ice that he shoved down his pants, and then he slumped on the floor by my mother's record albums.

"I'm gonna get blue balls from these encounters, I hope you know that," he muttered. "But each time we get closer to the brink. I just wish I didn't like your fiancé. I wish he wasn't such a good guy."

"Me too," I sighed, tying up my robe. I watched over his shoulder while he looked over some of the album covers: Dylan, Joplin, Iron Butterfly, The Mamas and The Papas sitting in a big claw-foot tub.

"I can't stand Bob Dylan," Mike complained. "He sings like somebody ran over his windpipe. Or they should run over it." He chuckled. "Record covers were so phony and posed back then. Check out these two guys."

He held up an album entitled *Gilberto e Gilberto, Canções do Amor.* The two men in question were wearing rust-colored turtlenecks, brown-striped pants and mod black sixties ankle boots while holding acoustic guitars and gazing longingly at something beyond the photographer.

"I think we're supposed to feel they're looking for love," I guessed.

"But what were they really looking at?" Mike laughed. "Some chick in a G-string? The food cart? A monkey riding a tricycle?"

"Wait a minute," I said, grabbing his shoulder and sitting up.

"What? Do you want to go at it again?" he asked, tossing the makeshift ice-pack aside. "Because I just need a second to warm up and I'll be ready. And you could always help the process along if you'd like."

"No, not that, stupid," I said, snatching the album from him and peering intently at the cover. Beyond the hokey pose, beyond the Canções do Amor, this record was from *Portugal* and these guys were named *Gilberto*. And it had been in my mother's possession. And when I looked closely at the darker Gilberto, I saw a familiar expression in the eyes—a serious but searching look I saw everyday. In the mirror.

"I'll bet that's my father," I whispered, my hands starting to tremble. "She always said he was either from Portugal or Spain and a few months ago when I got angry about something, she told me that I suddenly reminded her of him and that his name had been Gilberto. And I always imagined him playing a guitar—that was just intuitive. Isn't that crazy?"

Mike glanced at the album and then me, raising an eyebrow. "Well, he could look like your father…but maybe it's the other guy. He's named Gilberto too and he's got a guitar."

"No, he's all wrong," I objected. "He's got light brown hair and blue eyes…my mother had blue-green eyes too and no brown eye traits in her immediate family. Brown eyes are dominant so she had to have been with a darker man in order to produce me."

"She said Spain *or* Portugal," Mike reminded. "And both those countries are full of dark-eyed men."

"Named Gilberto?" I challenged. "That's not as common a name as José or Pablo or Juan. And she said Gilberto, she specifically said that."

"Just that she *thought* he was named Gilberto," Mike said, but he also reached over to stroke my hair. "This is important to you, isn't it? You used to act like you didn't care about your father but now you're all worked up and shaking even."

"Because he was like a vapor before," I said, trying not to cry. I always seemed to be crying in front of Mike. "He had no face or identity…I couldn't care about a totally anonymous person. But if this is him, my God, there he is—"

I broke off. I felt like one of the Seven Chinese Brothers who tried to swallow the ocean, but I did manage to hold back the tears.

"Why don't you look him up on-line?" Mike suggested, pointing to David's laptop that he refused to ever bring to the cabin, unless he was way behind on timesheets or had cases to review. "Maybe he's a famous musician. Maybe he's the best damn strummer Portugal's ever produced. Maybe he's a bum or maybe he's had a sex-change operation and become Gilberta. Whatever the case, I'd want to know."

We went in cyber-search of Gilberto Fonseca and found several others with that name, but honed it down to music and it looked like Gilberto and Gilberto had parted ways in the mid-seventies, but my Gilberto had moved to Ann Arbor, Michigan and opened a small restaurant/club named Fado where he still played on. Or at least where he had been playing as of 1999, which was when the article had been posted.

"Huh, looks like you've got the gene for Male Pattern Baldness," Mike said, noting the photograph with the article and how Gilberto Fonseca had lost most of his hair and become rather stooped around the shoulders. "Maybe you shouldn't bear my sons."

"Oh, leave him alone," I snapped. "Let's see what you look like in thirty years."

"Easy, sweetheart," he soothed. "Nobody wants to hurt your Daddy. In fact, why don't you call him now? Look him up in Ann Arbor and explain your situation. I'm sure he remembers your mother even if it was just a one-nighter."

"No," I objected, exiting the article and logging off. "Because did you see the part about how he has a wife and three other children? The only reason to get in touch would be pure selfishness, because he'd be all freaked about me and not sure what to do and it'd just cause trouble. It's not like I need bone marrow or blood or it's medically necessary. So forget it."

I slammed the laptop shut. My heart was racing but I was also so wiped out tired, like I had been through about five years worth of emotions in one hour.

"That's that then," Mike said. "You're letting it drop?"

"I think so." I sighed and then put the album back in the milk crate. "It's for the best."

"And what about me?" he asked, slipping his hands inside my robe again. "You're letting me drop too?"

I was so on the fence and ready to fall toward him, and if he had been the tiniest bit soothing and consoling about what had just happened he would have knocked me right down. But he was horny and tried for a quick kill by fingering me instead, and that was too rough and abrupt and I was able to make my decision.

"I'm sorry, Mike. I can't."

He put his head on my shoulder then drew his hand away. I looked at the cut-line of his hair against his strong neck, the down-turned corner of his mouth and something in my mind kept screaming: *DO it! Grab him, wrap your legs around him and don't let go!* But I shut that all out like I had closed the laptop and walked him to the foyer.

"You know this only makes me want you more," he said, now carrying an umbrella I had lent him since it hadn't stopped raining yet. "And it's gonna happen. It's almost planetary…things are moving toward each other and can't be stopped."

"Like the Titanic and the iceberg," I suggested, but he took unexpected offense.

"The Titanic was a tragedy and people died," he complained. "This is completely positive. Every time I'm with you I feel better about myself and about us and I know it's for the right reason."

I smoothed his still damp t-shirt and smiled. "Good night, Mike."

"I'll be back," he repeated while going down the stairs. "I'm relentless."

"He'll forget me in a week." I laughed quietly but without much humor, and then as quietly I closed the door.

CHAPTER 8

❀

I called my maybe-father's restaurant a few times after that but always hung up when someone answered. It was still in business, however, and when I was able to eek up the nerve to ask for Gilberto Fonseca, another man told me that he was in the middle of performing but did I want to leave a message? I could hear soft guitar strains and a feathery drum beat and glasses clinking in the background; I muttered no, no message, slammed the phone down then started bawling. This was ridiculous, of course, how some fifty-nine year old in Michigan had become so important, especially when I had been able to live my life just fine without him until now, and I almost hoped that if I ever did finally speak to him he'd say I never met your mother or I am totally infertile from excessive bicycling and my three other children are adopted, so take a walk, baby.

In the meantime I played his record over and over, mournfully and usually in the dark while lying on the floor. I was in a broody mood. I liked to burn a white jasmine candle while I listened to the plaintive duo; I put the candle on the floor next to me as I lay there and it was all so melancholy and poetic—until I nearly burned off my eyelashes from moving too close to the flame. But otherwise it was something I enjoyed in a pathetic self-indulgent way. When David asked me why I was so fond of that record I said that my mother had played it often when I was little and it reminded me of her. It wasn't that I wanted to lie to David; it was more that I didn't want the possibility of Gilberto Fonseca being my father to grow, and if only Mike and I knew about it then it would stay a secret. Because it had been discovered while Mike and I had been together in secret, doing illicit things on the same bed I slept with David in. Mike had taken out a *condom*, for God's sake. We had made serious erogenous contact. That had been full throttle wrong and it had been almost a minor miracle that seeing David's picture had stopped us.

June 21st was now a week away and again I started packing things old, new, borrowed and blue. I had also started making arrangements for the post-elopement party, which I figured we could have at the end of July so as to give people plenty of advance notice because a) I wanted really unique presents and not a bunch of toasters and blenders; and b) everybody was busier in the sum-mertime. Mike didn't seem to be as relentless as he'd promised and only stopped in once after our rendezvous, and since David was there he asked me to come back to the storage area with him.

"Don't worry, I'm not going to ravage you," he promised. I entered care-fully, twisting a wet dishtowel between my hands—I'm not sure why I brought that but maybe I thought I could use it as protection. I could flog him if he got out of line, cover his body with wet, slightly lemon-scented towel burns. But he didn't touch me, as promised, he just gave me the umbrella I had lent him and something wrapped in tissue paper.

"I won this on Ebay for $4," he said and I thought great, there's another link I don't want between us: he's an Ebay person. I had gotten both of my samo-vars from Ebay, one Russian and one Persian, for a song.

"Take it," he continued. "It's an incredible steal. It reminded me of you and I happened to be on-line when the auction came up. I was looking for some diamond chip cufflinks for Joe. You know his birthday's coming soon."

Inside the tissue paper was a red-flecked opal on a gold chain. "How pretty...but no, Mike," I whispered. "I can't accept this."

"Take it," he insisted. "It was four dollars including shipping. That's chump change."

"It's still not right," I said, though I allowed him to slip it around my neck. Don't look at him and don't remember how hard his abs and legs are, I thought. And other hard parts of him—don't think about those either.

"That looks great," he appraised. "Your skin really sets it off."

"You want it to remind me of you," I accused, suddenly getting angry. "And I'll see it every day and think about what could have been."

"Uh, no...I just wanted you to have an opal," he replied, holding up his hands like I'd pulled a gun. "Hold your fire, Lizzie. And if you're so sure about your decision, what do you care? What might have been is pointless, right?"

He walked off, using the back entrance. I called him a bastard and returned to the front of the tearoom, still muttering, but I couldn't quite bring myself to take the opal off. I was hot and it was hot and the ceiling fan overhead seemed to be spinning through water. I had put a CD from a local songwriter on and one of her refrains was particularly haunting:

> *He found the thread*
> *Fibrous and snaring*
> *And in his daring*
> *I found his bed.*
>
> *He was much more*
> *Than I demanded*
> *Have to be candid*
> *It works for me.*

I fingered the fine chain of the opal and listened, served somebody a golden raisin scone and a cup of Ti Kuan Yin and then I looked at David, who was at the window corner table working on his laptop. He was tanned from a week-end at the cabin and had gotten a close-cropped buzz cut so that he looked younger and slightly bewildered; he glanced up and flashed me a peace sign, then kept typing. I smiled and felt the tense uncertain knot in me relax. Just stick with David, I now thought instead. It's only another week…just keep following him and everything will be fine.

My brother Pete was acting weirder than usual and kept saying he had something important to tell me, but he couldn't talk over the phone or at Samovar or in my apartment—we had to go far away from other people, apparently. That evening as I was closing he stopped by (it was Gemma's day off—Pete was gloomily avoiding her because she had started dating another musician) and said he wanted to take a little ride.

"Why?" I asked, scooping a loose earring up off the floor and tossing it into the lost and found box by the cash register. "Are you going to kill me? I don't think you can do it, Pete. I don't think you have the stuff."

"Ha, you're a riot," he said without laughing. "Spleen rupturing funny. This is serious, Liz. Prep yourself."

We drove to Montrose Harbor and looked at the pale night sky along the water. I hated his car even more now because he still hadn't had the exhaust problem fixed and it reminded me of driving to the hospital when my mother had had her heart attack. I stepped out to get some fresh air and wander along the shoreline while he followed.

'Shit," he murmured, stroking his goatee. "I hate to lay this on you but I have to, I can't not say anything anymore. You need to know the truth."

My God, he's gay, I thought, and suddenly many things about him made sense: the evasiveness with women, the emotional retreats, the extreme closeness to this guy named Balthazar who rarely spoke and seemed like a mental zombie. I asked him if that was the case and told him that was completely fine, I had no issue with it.

"*I'm* gay—yeah, right!" he yelled, upsetting a bunch of nearby seagulls into flight. "You are so looking through the wrong end of the telescope…oh fuck, forget it."

Back in the car I tried to pin him down but he shook his head and kept silent. I thought about the wrong end of the telescope and what that could mean and figured that that was the reverse of what you should be seeing. Since *I* wasn't gay and if I was I would probably know that fact myself and wouldn't need him to inform me, I then thought maybe he'd gotten some girl pregnant. Or he already had a child. No, more likely he had gotten someone pregnant and was going to have to deal with fatherhood. I could think of few men as poorly equipped as my brother to have a baby. He could barely find his keys every morning and if you asked him to be someplace or do something because you really needed him to, he refused to show up. He would surely be moving to Oregon or Vancouver now, to avoid being around at the time of birth. Pete's general mantra was still out of sight, out of mind.

"Well, thanks for the ride," I said when he dropped me off. "Are you going to Joe's party Saturday?"

Joe's parents were throwing him a thirtieth birthday party at their house in Chicago Heights. I had been invited and so had David and Pete. David claimed he had a brief to write and most likely wouldn't be able to go, so I had hoped that I could use Pete as a buffer like a dishtowel and not have to worry about ending up in a closet with Mike.

"Are *you* going?" he asked, looking at me in a strange way. "With David?"

"David's doubtful," I said. "But I'll go if you do. I'm sure the food will be great. And Joe's girlfriend is finally coming in from Paris."

"Oh, yeah, the girlfriend from Paris," Pete echoed. "I'd love to check her out."

"She's Joe's girlfriend," I reminded.

"I'm sure she is," he said, and then he agreed to come along which meant that the odds of him actually showing up were about 10 to 1.

Just to spite me, however, Pete showed. I left David with a headache and two-thirds of his brief remaining and we traveled far south to Chicago Heights. I was a little anxious about the party because I didn't trust myself to stay away from Mike and knew that some of my motivation for going was to see what his parents were like and where he had grown up, but as I drove to the Heights I started to not care and to just enjoy the evening. I've always loved Italian neighborhoods and the statues of the Virgin Mary and Jesus in front of the homes, the smell of garlic and tomatoes from the restaurants or yeast and flour from the bakeries. The churches, the big cars, the old men puffing fat stinky cigars. Mike's house was a split-level with a statue of St. Francis on its lawn; his father looked more like Joe, twinkly-eyed with glasses, and his mother was still something of a knockout in her red 1950s dress with the cinched waist and matching red sandals. She had huge brown eyes and a megawatt smile and she gave me a hug and said she'd heard all about me and David and this young man, meaning Pete, who looked like he wanted to take a dive into the nearest clump of shrubbery. Pete can't handle excessive displays of affection.

Nonetheless he was dragged in and through the house to the back yard, where colored lanterns had been strung and Sinatra music played and people were eating and drinking and smoking informally. I followed, setting Joe's present on the living room table with the others. Pete had shown up empty-handed but I brought a tin of the Russian tea Joe reminded me of (like David), and a black silk turtleneck. Mrs. Catapano introduced us around and made us heap our plates with stuffed shells and antipasto and bread and calamari salad, and then she brought us over to Mike, who was mixing drinks for everyone. Mike had on a tan linen suit with a white open-collared shirt and he looked fantastic. I shook my head, smiling; I couldn't help it.

"Pete wants a beer, and preferably Corona," Mike pronounced, throwing him a bottle, which Pete caught deftly. "Now this lovely lady might want a glass of rosé…is that a good guess, Liz?"

"Maybe white wine on ice," I said. "If you have any."

"Uh oh, I'm wrong…have to take a shot." Mike poured himself a dose of Jagermeister and drank it down. "That's the rule here…if I screw up on my psychic bartending, I have to take a shot of something. Or if I get the drink right, I have to take a shot. I'm drinking to forget. Only I can't remember what I was supposed to forget." He pointed in my direction. "Oh yeah, I think it's you."

It occurred to me then that Mike was kind of in the bag, which was surprising. He had never come across as a big drinker. Maybe scotch on the rocks, a martini, a few glasses of wine at dinner, but he wasn't chronic. My brother was somebody who got hammered on a regular basis, but Mike had a business to run and he liked to keep in shape and play basketball and it seemed like alcohol would just slow him down.

"Come stand behind here with me and help," Mike urged. "I like your dress. And your necklace."

I was wearing a slip dress with a climbing rose pattern, so I had left the opal on because it went with the red of the petals.

"I can't," I said. "I have to say hi to Joe. And I can't leave Pete alone, he's socially retarded."

"But you're just retarded," Pete countered, pushing me behind the bar with Mike and then making a beeline for Joe and his father and a blonde girl sitting on the couch. I knew the girl was Joe's fiancée because of her full French lips and how she used her eyes. Mike's mother passed and saw me standing with her son and smiled.

"Honey, tell him to knock off the boozing," she said, patting at her hair in the hall mirror. "Michael doesn't listen to me anymore, he's terribly disrespectful."

Mike took a swig of vodka. "Hey, I love you Gloria Catapano," he yelled back. "You little foxy ma-mma! You go show 'em how it's done."

His mother winked and moved on. Sinatra was replaced by Tom Jones and lots of clapping. I could smell several forms of alcohol on Mike and feel the collective heat of them working through his body.

"Did you eat anything?" I asked. "Or is this sloshing around in an empty stomach?"

He swallowed some grappa then gagged. "Blaaaggh! Holy frig…that's wicked stuff," he laughed. He slipped his arm around my waist and swayed back and forth to *Delilah*. "I'm so glad you're here, Liz. Have a shot."

"No more shots," I said. "How about some coffee?"

"How about *tea*, Ms. Samovar. Tea for two and you for me, huh?" He leaned over to my ear, whispering. "How about I take you upstairs, rip off your dress and do you right in the bathroom?"

I have to admit that I knew I should leave at that point and join the others, but I didn't. Even in such a polluted state I liked the warmth of his breath on my neck and how he felt swaying beside me. "Why not do it here, Mike? Why waste time going upstairs?"

"You want to? You want to give these people some real entertainment?" He tried to raise my dress but I slapped him down and then I saw him staring uneasily at the ricotta-laden shells and fried rings of calamari on my buffet plate.

"I don't feel so great. I need to puke," he decided. "You know, like in ancient Rome. People would go to these big tiled rooms, stick feathers down their throats to throw up and empty out their stomachs. Then they'd start gorging and drinking again. Everybody did it…crazy frigging Romans. One more for the road," he said, grabbing a bottle of anisette, filling a cordial glass and draining it with drunken elegance. He then touched the opal around my neck and smiled.

"Lizzie," he murmured solemnly. "We have a dynamic, we have something and you won't let it happen. It's more than just wanting to do it…it's like sometimes I think of things I want to tell you, things I see or whatever, but then I can't because it's not right for me to call you or see you all the time. And it's such a waste. It's like the dead letter part of the post office, you know? Things lying around unsaid, undelivered. Things that never get to be."

I looked at him in awe over that comment and over the fact that tears were glistening in his eyes, but then he laughed and went tramping up the stairs to make himself hurl. Cake was being served on the deck along with plastic flute glasses of champagne; Joe blew out his thirty candles and there was more clapping and toasting and now we were listening to Johnny Mathis. I wandered around with my champagne looking at various photos of Mike and Joe, Mr. and Mrs. Catapano and Gina, the younger sister; Mike with feathered hair and an earring, Joe looking almost scrawny—it seemed like he hadn't filled out until the end of high school. Baby pictures, school pictures, wedding portraits. In the kitchen Mrs. Catapano had slipped off her sparkly sandals and was tiptoe in her stocking feet hugging Joe around the neck and wailing, "My Joey is thirty! How did that *happen*…Joseph Anthony, where did the time go?"

I chatted with Mr. Catapano about working at City Hall in the death records section, which was strangely more interesting and less creepy than it sounded; then I tried to talk to a very old toothless lady who was sucking on Jordan almonds and who spoke about three words of English. And then some keyed-up redhead enveloped in perfume and a sequined dress tight as a sausage casing accosted me and told me how she'd dated both Mike and his best friend Paulie senior year, only she'd been stupid enough to choose Paulie and now she was married to him and he'd become a fat football-watching slob.

"See?" she yelled, pointing to a chunky man drinking a Heineken in the corner. "There's the useless sack of shit. You think he can even get it up anymore? Think again. I wish a lightning bolt would blast right through that window and blow him off the face of the earth. Meanwhile, Mikey is still so *gorgeous*. Every time I see him I want to drop to my knees, you know, and turn back the time machine."

She was wearing false eyelashes and one of them was dangling precariously. Although the eyelash was fascinatingly pendulous, she was moving in too close so I pretended to have to go look for something in the glove compartment of my car. I then saw my brother coming to the car to smoke a joint and ripped into him for his outrageous flirting with Vivienne. They had practically been all over each other right in front of Joe, who seemed oddly passive.

"I know she's French but control yourself," I snapped. "Since when are you such a ladies' man anyway? And put that out—can't you live without weed for one night?"

He inhaled deeply then pinched off the glowing tip and pocketed the roach once it had cooled. "Look," he said, still exhaling. "I have to tell you this now because it'll explain a lot of people's behavior." He turned to me with unusual calm and for once did not mumble, stutter or stammer. "David is gay, Liz, and so is Joe. Or they're bi or whatever, but I saw them in bed together when I was at the cabin. And it wasn't just because Joe didn't want to sleep on the couch."

"You *what*?" I said, turning toward him sharply and in doing so my elbow hit the horn and we both jumped. "Were you fucked up at the time? Doing mushrooms or something?"

"I was utterly lucid," he maintained. "I got up early in the morning to go fishing and saw them through the window. It wasn't just sleeping, it was um, embracing and other stuff. That's why I had to tell you. Some strange shit is going on between them and it's heavy duty."

I felt like suddenly like I was Alice in Wonderland and I had fallen into a screaming swirling vortex that had no bottom. The two of them together, *embracing*…was he trying to pull some horrible practical joke? Or was any of this really happening and was it only a nightmare and in a few hours I'd have to get up to go to Joe's party and wrap his black sweater. My brother took my arm and pressed his fingers against it gently.

"Hey," he prodded. "Are you okay? Should we leave? By the way, that's why I'm hitting on Vivienne. She's incredibly hot and it's a sham marriage, even though Joe claimed it wasn't. It's a sham for the green card and to fool his family. She likes him as a friend a lot and they worked it out together. Once I told her what I'd seen, she backed it up with more facts."

This was just too much to absorb. My mind felt like a broken slide projector, with all these images of happy times with David mixed up with clues I had obviously missed: Joe visiting the cabin, Joe's depression, David's mood swings and David's sudden urge to get married, the mystery phone call from months ago. Joe had wanted to tell me about David, that's who it had been. He had at least *tried*—I'm not sure why but that meant a great deal to me, and therefore I didn't try to run him over when he came down the driveway carrying his two year old niece to his sister's car.

Poor Joe. I watched him ease the sleeping little girl into the backseat so carefully then kiss his sister goodbye. I would be all right; I could feel the air coming back to my lungs and the blood starting to move again throughout my body, but Joe had deeper issues. He had this family who loved him so much but who would probably go ballistic if he were to tell them he was gay, and he had had to import a fake fiancée while at the same time deal with the fact that someone he had fallen in love with was engaged to me. Someone also leading a double life.

"God," I murmured. "He's one incredible actor."

"Who?" Pete asked, nodding to Joe through the windshield. "Him?"

"No. David." I started to cry then checked myself. I felt like I needed to churn up a lot of anger and action now, not sadness and tears. "I mean he certainly could act in bed. He never had a problem there."

"Maybe he's into both sexes," Pete suggested tactfully. "Some people are. Mom was like that, every now and then. She—"

"Never mind, spare me the details," I interrupted. "I've just gotten Mom into a good place in my head, let's not scramble the picture anymore."

Joe was walking past and tapped on my window, which I had quickly closed for fear I might start screaming.

"You're not leaving already?" he asked us both. "Liz, I can't believe you gave me that turtleneck—it actually makes me look cool. International cool, you know? You have great taste."

He was smiling and his eyes crinkled at the corners like they always did. I knew then that Joe really liked and cared about me, because he wasn't one to cover up his feelings well, I had seen that in the past, but he had never shown anything but kindness and friendship where I was concerned. Of course he had also had a secret affair with my almost-husband, but then I was willing to bet that David had been the aggressor in that and the one to break it off.

"I need to talk to you, Joe," I said, and even though I tried to keep my voice calm, I knew that he knew that I knew. "Can we go someplace alone?"

"Yeah, sure," he said, but he looked like he might be sick. He opened the door and helped me out of the car and we went back toward the house.

"I'm ready to go whenever you are, Liz," Pete called, and while I heard him and I nodded in response, he seemed like he was miles away and the only two people who really existed were Joe and myself and the difficult words we were about to exchange.

CHAPTER 9

❀

I talked to Joe in the bathroom adjoining the room he and Mike had used to share, now a catchall storage area with just a few vestiges of its former tenants. Including its former tenant, Mike, who had passed out on his old twin bed and was sleeping off three hours of participatory bartending. We locked the door and I sat tensely on the tub ledge while Joe told me about David, Vivienne and all sort of things. High school experiences, Catholic guilt, lots of secrecy. David was indeed bisexual but Joe was gay. David was serious in his wanting to marry me but would have affairs every now and then even though he was privately trying to put himself through aversion therapy not to.

"Like what?" I demanded. "He'd wear a testicular electric shock device and zap himself every time he felt something for a man?"

"It was more psychological," Joe said. "He would think of his parents and how upset they'd be if they knew, or he thought about a gay partner at the firm who was pretty much ostracized and who had died of AIDS."

"Oh God," I murmured, remembering that man and covering my face. "This is terrible. This is so messed up."

Joe shifted around unhappily on the fluffy yellow bathmat. "No, what I did to you is terrible. I hate myself, Liz, I swear. I should have stopped it…even when David told me he didn't want to have a long-term relationship, that he wanted to be with you and whatever happened between us was like a last fling. But I didn't. And I wouldn't blame you if you never spoke to me again."

"Look," I said, still not quite knowing what to think. "I can't go over that now in too much depth. Whatever happened happened, and maybe it was almost meant to. So don't hate yourself."

"David said we both needed to keep it together, he said, we were both in situations where we couldn't be open about the way we are," Joe went on regardless. "And I didn't want to get all fatal attraction on him even though I care so
much, I can't get past it. But then my brother started telling me how he felt
about you and how he couldn't have a chance because you were engaged. That
you were too moral to cheat and…." He trailed off. "Jeez, I don't know. It's just
that I've never seen Mike like this and it seemed wrong to let the whole thing
go on."

"But your brother was worked up over Gemma too," I sighed. "He probably
likes somebody new every two weeks. That's why I couldn't get involved with
him, really. I knew it would be over so quickly and all the time I'd spent with
David would be ruined. Of course, if I'd known that David was having affairs
with *men* behind my back, it might have been a different story. What a stupid
ass he is."

"He's not stupid, he's just conflicted," Joe said. "You've met his parents,
you've seen where he works. Doesn't it make sense? Can you see any of them
dealing well with a bisexual?"

I glanced at Joe irritably because I didn't want to be having empathy pains
for anyone. I also hated him for a moment when I imagined him kissing and
touching David, but then the harsh bitterness passed and I just slumped forward.

"I can see why he's conflicted, yes," I said. "I'll give him that much. But he
should have told me earlier. I've invested myself in this too, you know. It's not
all about his problems."

"He wanted so much to be with you, though, Liz," Joe persisted. "He told
me that if anyone could pull him through and keep him on the right side, it'd
be you."

"Oh, shut up—who's to say what side is right or wrong," I snapped, losing
my anger and starting to cry while Joe sat on the tub ledge too and gingerly
patted my back. I think he was afraid to touch me; that I might throw him off.
There was a knock on the door and Joe and I looked at each other, then Joe
handed me a guest towel to dry my eyes and went to answer. It was Pete, carrying a cup of hot tea.

"Hey, what's happening?" he said, handing the cup to me. "This is all Mrs.
C. had, just Lipton in bags. But then again, there's nothing like the classics. Joe,
you'd better get downstairs because Vivienne's pretty ripped on champagne
and becoming chatty. I tried to tell her to fermez la bouche and she almost
smacked me." He grinned. "She's a wildcat."

"I'll be right there," Joe said. "Take her outside—tell her you're going to buy her an Italian beef," he added. "I'm not being gross, she really likes Italian beef sandwiches with all the peppers and stuff."

Pete left and Joe guided me up off the tub to show me something in his old room. Beyond Mike, who was muttering and cursing about people tramping in and out while he was trying to sleep, he pointed to a poster for the movie *Serpico* and then to my cup of tea. And then he brought me into the hall, closing the door behind him.

"Earlier today, when we were getting ready for the party, Mike looked at that poster and told me it depressed him," Joe elaborated. "He said there's this part in *Serpico* where Al Pacino makes a cup of tea and one of the other cops says that he never trusts any man who drinks tea…and it's an interesting character thing that shows how different Serpico is from the other detectives. They all drink coffee like most guys in the sixties did, but he drank tea and they thought he was a weirdo and suspicious."

"Your brother was depressed because of that?" I asked. "That's the whole focus of the movie: Frank Serpico is a rebel."

"It's the *tea*," Joe laughed, shaking his head. "That's what Mike wanted to relay. He wanted to call and tell you right that minute…I don't know why he was so caught up in it. You're really under his skin…he says he has things to tell you all the time but he can't."

"I know," I said, remembering the dead letter comment and things that could never be. "God, he's driving me insane too."

"I'm sorry, Liz," Joe then said. "I swear, I really am."

Joe paused at the foot of the stairs and looked at me with such guilt, I couldn't stand it; I had to put the tea down on the landing and hold his face between my hands. "Don't be," I whispered. "You're fine, there's nothing wrong. All you did was bring out the truth, and at just the right time. So don't worry." I smiled, adjusting his new oval wire-rimmed glasses. "And you're adorable too, I hope you know that. If you were straight and I had to choose between you and your brother it'd be pretty tough."

He gripped my hand for a second then picked up my tea. "It's too soon to know of course but I hope you stay in our family, Liz," he said. "Good luck. You're gonna need it with Mike, I'm sure."

"Are you planning to tell him?" I asked before we rejoined the others. "About what happened and who you really are?"

"I don't know," he said, his eyes getting guilty and fearful again. "How can I? How can I tell any of these people?"

"Very slowly, like diffusing a bomb," I advised, and then I went to find my brother, who was half-heartedly fighting off Vivienne's fierce attempts to fellate him in my car.

Having pried the great lovers apart, I drove Pete home. Pete said that I could stay with him instead of having to deal with David, but I couldn't think that far ahead, I only wanted to talk to David and hear his version of it all. He had clearly been tipped off by Joe, however, before I got there because when I walked in he was sitting hunched over the dining room table chewing off the inside of his lower lip.

"Liz, I'm sorry, you have to believe me," he said. "This—"

I was so tired. Again, being a Waring blender of emotions had worn me out and I kept walking and went to the bedroom. David followed. He started talking about cross-wired feelings for men and women and things just happening with Joe, and still wanting to get married and couldn't I understand and hadn't we been through so much with each other. I was listening while undressing and then combing my hair, but suddenly I cleared everything off my dressing table in a single swoop of fury. I had seen that in an old movie once and I remembered thinking it was an impressive gesture but who would ever have reason to be so dramatic? Now I knew. It felt stupid and satisfying at the same time. It scared David out of the room, which was good because I didn't want to hear him anymore. I could listen tomorrow or the day after that—the problem wasn't something with a deadline.

I moved my half-packed bridal suitcase away from the foot of the bed and realized that I had been stopped from marrying him twice and somebody had to have been looking out for me. I picked my mother's amber beads off the ground and said thanks, Beth, but then I also picked up the photo of David standing in front of the antique store and it made me start crying again. I almost went to be with him to try to perhaps work things out, but I put Gilberto Fonseca's record on instead and lay on the rug listening. There was still debris from the dresser—change, a lipstick tube, a bobby pin—underneath me but it didn't matter. I just liked hearing the guitars and watching the black disk go around and around the old turntable, and by the time the needle had reached the center, I was dead to the world.

In the morning I woke fairly early, showered, dressed and snuck past David, who was sleeping on the foldout with a pillow over his head. I went to the tea-room even though I had opted not to open it on Sundays during the summer, both to give myself and Gemma and Thea a break and because more people went away on summer weekends. Still, I went over there because it was a refuge and so I could clean and mop and scour and divert my thoughts while drinking Earl Grey on ice with honey and a big wedge of orange floating to the top of the glass. That was my hot weather get it together power tea drink. Invented that morning. Necessity being the mother of invention, of course.

Around midday when I figured Mike's hangover would have subsided, I went to the Napoli and saw Joe, who was getting ready to close too—they rarely stayed open past three on Sundays. Joe greeted me solemnly when I walked in.

"How are you?" he asked. I said good enough. I said I knew he had called David to give him advance warning last night but Joe claimed that that was for my sake.

"I didn't want him to do anything stupid when you came through the door," he said. "Like yell at you for not paying the phone bill or be standing there naked with a can of whipped cream."

"That would not have been wise," I agreed.

Joe wiped the green marble counter nervously. "Did you talk it out with him?"

"I didn't have the strength. Or the patience. You know, Joe," I reflected, taking a few incredibly buttery Italian bakery cookies dipped in chocolate from a plate and munching them slowly. "I don't have as much patience as I used to. Or understanding. Like if this had happened a year ago, I would have stayed up all night with David and talked it through, come to some resolution or arrangement, whatever. Now I just wanted to get the hell out of there. I wonder what's happening to me."

"Maybe you want more from someone else," Joe said. I glanced around the café area and smiled wryly.

"Where is your brother anyhow?" I asked.

"In his apartment. He was useless today. He got down here around eleven a.m. then left at one. He's still hung-over. He doesn't even remember me driving him home and dragging his drunken ass upstairs."

Joe lived on the ground level of the Caffè Napoli, behind the storefront, whereas Mike had the top floor. I asked Joe where Vivienne had gone and he said to visit some friends.

"Where did you meet her anyway?" I asked.

"Before Mike and I opened this place I used to work at The Green Mill bartending. She came in there when she was on a student visa…she was going to school at the Art Institute. For fashion design. We hit it off and she kept coming back, and then we worked out an arrangement."

Fashion design. No wonder she had been wearing a top that looked like it was made out of fuchsia Saran Wrap last night, I thought.

"Why do people even emigrate from France?" I wondered aloud. "Especially if they're into fashion. Isn't Paris the fashion capital of the world?"

Joe shrugged. "It's one of them. New York is another…it depends on your point of view. Plus she wanted to tick off her old boyfriend by changing citizenship. He hates America."

"Ah," I nodded. "Excellent motivation. Give us your tired, your hungry, your spiteful. Are you still planning to go through with it? Because if you are, don't sign over any property or assets. Sorry, I've been hanging around a lawyer for too long," I added. "Force of habit."

Joe stroked his chin. "I don't know. My ma called this morning and said she didn't like Vivienne, that she seemed *loose*. But then she doesn't know the whole story." He smiled. "My mother asked if you had any sisters, by the way. For me and Mike to marry."

"I have a sister but she'd condemn you to hell. She's a Baptist convert," I answered. "And sorry, but even with the recent revelations I could see myself married to you before being with Mike. Although of course I have to go find him now. It's a moth to flame thing. Compulsion beyond reason."

"No, I think you just like each other," Joe said, giving a last polish to the marble then knocking the pulp out of the juicer, probably calming himself with these little rituals like I had calmed down earlier by cleaning the tearoom. "Liz?" he called, just as I was about to head for the stairs that led to Mike's apartment. "Do you think I should tell my mother?"

He seemed to be picking up some edgy determination and I wanted to encourage that. Having seen his mother and how much she loved him, I felt she could handle it; she would be shocked, of course, but in the end would accept and ease the change into her life.

"If you want to, then you should," I said. "She's a great lady and seems to have a big heart. Even your father will learn to deal with it. I think Mike's going to be the most explosive, just because he'll feel so confused and thrown off."

"Once I tell her I'll have to tell him," Joe sighed. "Ma can't keep anything secret. And if he finds out from her he'll really be upset."

"Maybe I can tell him," I offered, after thinking for a moment. Thinking about returning to the apartment and dealing with David, which I didn't want to do, as opposed to being with Mike, which I did want…but in a different place. Like Ann Arbor, Michigan. Even though I didn't want to speak to my maybe-father I wanted to at least see him, just sit at a darkened table in his restaurant and watch him play. Ann Arbor was only about four hours away and I wondered if Mike would come with me. Then perhaps we could be together and see if we had any reason to carry on. I knew it was quite soon after the whole David issue, but it was almost like I needed to be irrational and throw myself into the next available bed. I had always been a rational person and in the past would have allowed for grieving and thinking and retrospection, but now I wanted to be reckless. I wanted to do two impulsive and passionate things at once instead of analyzing them both for months and wondering what might happen *if*.

"No!" Joe urged, hurrying toward me. "Don't tell Mike now…I can't handle that and he's got a major headache, he's in a bad enough mood."

"I meant maybe he and I could take a short trip and I'll tell him elsewhere," I said. "Away from here, hopefully when he's in a better mood." I explained my plan. "Can you manage without him for a few days?"

"I can ask my mother to fill in for him," Joe said. "That'll give me time alone with her too. She likes working here every once in a while. Getting out of the Heights and being in the city, flirting with cops when they come in for lunch. She thinks it's a kick."

"All right then," I said. "You'll have to talk to Vivienne too but I'm sure she can find another green card guy. Even my brother might volunteer…she's really assertive with him; he seems to like that. Now we just have to make sure that Mike wants to take a few days off with me."

"Why wouldn't he?" Joe laughed.

"I don't know. He might have other plans. He might have changed his mind. He—"

"Mike will go," Joe interrupted. "I'd be willing to put money down on it. Here…." He threw me a set of keys, which I almost dropped but caught right before they hit the terrazzo floor. "He could be sleeping again and won't hear you knock. And if he's not in the main area look up on the roof. He's got a staircase leading to the rooftop and he'll either be out there in the hammock or on the wicker lounge."

He was on the wicker lounge with a washcloth over his forehead, unshaven and wearing only a pair of Bermuda shorts. I liked the unshaven look and the bare chest but his eyes were puffy and he seemed to have trouble using his mouth. There was none of the usual expressive animated Mike or the sense of hard tension in his body. He just looked trashed. I noticed that he had a tattoo of the Playboy bunny logo on his left bicep and tried not to visibly wince. It didn't seem possible that I was thinking of involving myself with any guy with a tattoo like that, or any guy who openly supported Hugh Hefner's Pajamas and Pipe enterprise. But still I went and sat by his side.

I liked the rooftop and what he had done with it: white Christmas lights strung here and there, big terracotta-potted plants, candles, a bistro type table and chair set with a Cinzano umbrella, the hammock and lounge. As I had passed through his apartment I had noticed a predominantly black and tan theme with a few shrewdly placed antiques and ethnic items—pretty good taste for a single man.

"This is a surprise," he said, taking the washcloth off his forehead and wiping his face with it. "What brings you here?"

"I'm checking on you from last night," I answered, wanting to lean over and kiss his chest but restraining myself. Just a little while longer, I thought. He wasn't in top form now anyway. "You were pretty blotto."

"Yeah, that was stupid," he sighed. "I can't drink like that anymore...I'm thirty-three. For one thing it's not good for the body and for another, you should just know better at this age."

"Well, we all lapse sometimes," I said. "For whatever reason."

He groped around for his sunglasses in the glare of the afternoon light and since they were beyond his reach under the lounge chair, I handed them to him.

"Thanks. So how'd you like my folks?" he asked.

"They were nice. The food was delicious and it was fun to see your house and your sister and your great-aunt Josephine. And your old girlfriend who hates her husband because he's a fat slob and wants you back again."

Mike laughed grimly. "Give me a break. First of all, she's embellishing the truth...she wasn't a girlfriend, she was somebody you knew you could get action out of without going to much trouble. And second of all, she's worn Paulie down into what he is. He's given up because she's always carping. So he eats and drinks and tunes her out."

"Fascinating," I said.

"Don't be sarcastic," he muttered.

"I'm not," I insisted. "I'm just thinking of people who got married right out of high school...can you imagine that? I've changed so much since then and you probably have too."

"I'm a lot different," he agreed. "It's like I've done a one-eighty. Back then I basically wanted to get laid, make money and have fun. That was my triple objective in life."

"So how are you different now?" I joked.

"My skin's cleared up," he quipped back. "And I'm pining after women like you."

"Wo*men*?" I repeated. "There's a group of us?"

"As many as I can find," he said. He swallowed what was left of a glass of ice water then chewed on the remaining cubes. "Wow, that's brutal," he chuckled. "All that crunching going through my head in stereo."

I sat and watched him chew, noted a vein pulsing in his throat, then asked abruptly if he wanted to go to Ann Arbor and why we should make the trip.

"Are you serious?" He glanced around and behind the chair. "This is a joke, right? You're suddenly over with David? I hope you didn't do this for me…you didn't do this for me, right?" he exacted, but he almost sounded like he wanted that to have been the reason.

"We had extenuating circumstances," I said, and I left it at that. "Do you want to drive up tomorrow? It's not too long a ride. We can take my car, I don't mind."

A long pause stretched between us. Now came the acid test, I thought; now I would find out whether he was more turned on by pursuing the forbidden than actually having a chance. There were men like that who just wanted to seduce or lure you away, and then once they had you they lost interest. I wondered whether he'd make an excuse or say he had other plans. I didn't like the damn sunglasses either, since I couldn't read his eyes, and I was about to pull them off when he said sure, he'd love to go.

"Good," I said, standing up yet feeling wobbly, perhaps at the thought of soon being in a moving vehicle and perhaps a motel with Mike, but I had to go through with it since I was the one who had come up with the idea in the first place. "I guess we could leave around noon."

"Let's take my car," he said. "I need the leg room."

"Fine." I waved goodbye and started to walk away.

"Hold on," he objected. "That's it…you're just taking off? I mean, I know I look like I'm half-dead but give me a peck on the cheek or something. I can't be taking off on an overnight trip with you with that kind of attitude."

I kissed him on the cheek and let my lips brush against the stubble around his jaw. He slid his hands down over my thighs and pulled me in a bit more for another kiss, but then he let me go.

"You're being a gentleman," I said. "That's sweet."

"It's for my own sake. I'm a mess," he smiled. "I'd probably pass out midway through. And I still must stink from all the crap I drank…I can smell myself even."

"You smelled worse last night," I assured him. "Now it's more skin than gin. Nice clean and showered skin."

"Thanks," he said, releasing my arm so that I could leave. "And thanks for asking me to go with you."

"You were there when I found the Gilberto record and looked him up," I said. "And no one else knows…well, I had to tell Joe but otherwise it's just you and me."

"We have a secret together," Mike laughed. "I like secrets."

I'll bet you won't like certain secrets, I thought, especially the ones coming at you on this trip, but I just said goodbye and told him I'd be back tomorrow at noon and left him there on the rooftop, all the leaves of the plants and the edge of the Cinzano umbrella rustling softly in the breeze.

CHAPTER 10

❀

Before we left for Michigan David said he wanted to talk to me about living arrangements and other business, so we sat in the kitchen at a raw and tender 7 a.m. discussing which bills were in whose name, who would keep the apartment (me), who would take the couch, television, DVD player, bed and dining room set (him), and the usual difficult but practical matters. I gave him the ruby and pearl engagement ring. He refused to accept it and we both looked at it lying there on the table miserably, but I couldn't take it back.

"You know this is a nightmare," he said, pressing hard on his temples, and it all hit me at that point—the finality of the situation—because just a few days ago I would have reached over and rubbed his temples for him while sitting on his lap. My eyes watered and I shook my head.

"It doesn't have to be a nightmare but I can't be with you anymore, I'm sorry."

He reached across the table and took my hand. "Please. What if I swear to you that it will never happen again…if I sign some kind of contract, like a prenuptial agreement?"

"Are you insane?" I laughed. "You can't sign a *contract* for that. David, I'm not going to be your beard, I can't do it. I need more."

"You wouldn't be my beard and you would have more," he retorted. "You had it all along…this was just a stupid act of bad judgment on my part. What if it'd been a woman? Would you have forgiven me for that?"

"I don't know," I said. "It's an interesting question hypothetically but in *reality* it wasn't a woman and it's a whole other situation. And you were drawn into being with Joe for a reason, so maybe you should find out why that was. You knew it would be risky, you knew you might get caught, but you kept on with it. You even invited him to the cabin while I was there, for God's sake. Talk about pushing the envelope."

"Look, I thought I could invite Joe as a friend because it was over between us…I wanted to help him out because he was upset and depressed, but then you left!" he yelled. "You left me alone with him."

"So am I supposed to be a human shield for every man you feel attracted to?" I yelled back. "Be constantly by your side keeping you hetero? I don't think so. To be honest, I think you seriously care about Joe and that's why you asked him up there. You're not a sleazy person who likes to mix his lovers up socially and you don't have casual affairs. I think he cares about you too and you're a good match for each other."

"No, no, NO!" David shouted, banging his palm against the tabletop. "I'm not walking down that path, with the gay domestic partner and the snickering and fag jokes behind your back even though the law says you can't discriminate, because believe me, the discrimination still goes on. And my mother pretending that she's all liberal and with it and asking us for decorating advice…I swear, I'd rather jump off a bridge. Seriously."

"Don't jump off any bridges," I urged. "Please."

"Why do you care," he muttered. "I figure you'd want to push me first."

I looked at him sitting in his usual place at the table, ticking off items on a list that he had made regarding "Liz Things"—I could see the heading he had written at the top of the page. He was wearing a watch I had given him for Christmas. His wrist had a slight oil burn from when we had made homemade tempura last week. My eyes filled with tears again and through the magnification of them he became unbearably clear and close, just for a moment.

"I care because I was supposed to spend the rest of my life with you," I said. "It's hard to switch it off."

"Then don't," he pleaded. "I will try every way I can to make you happy, I swear. Liz, give me another chance."

I sighed and put my head on the table. "No, I can't," I said. "You don't want to do it for me, you want to do it for your reputation."

"That's not true—"

"David, no," I repeated numbly. "It's not going to happen. Let it drop."

"You just need more time," he decided, finishing his coffee and putting the list back into his briefcase. "To deal with everything, but then we'll work it out. I know we will."

"You're delusional," I said, still with my head on the table until I noticed a small pile of mail I'd been ignoring and how one of the envelopes had come from my sister Amy. She had sent an announcement of her newborn son Nathaniel Joshua with a photo of her in the delivery bed holding the baby while her husband beamed at her side. Superimposed on the photo were the words *Nathaniel: Gift of God* in cursive lettering, and the only problem was that the baby was the tiniest most diabolical creature I had ever seen. There was just something about the too bright blue eyes, the twist of the pink mouth, the swirls of hair that looked like little devil horns. And if you looked closely, that baby was already giving the world the middle finger. That baby's first gesture to the world had been to say I am hellfire, watch for my wrath.

"Is it my imagination or does Nathaniel Joshua look possessed?" I asked, showing it to David, and despite the intensity of our previous discussion he laughed.

"Your nephew has demon seed written all over him," David confirmed. "He'll be sacrificing goats before he can even talk. By the first grade he'll be causing minor earthquakes and spontaneous fires. Yet he will walk the earth as a televangelist." I laughed too then we stared at each other awkwardly.

"Do you see how it still is with us, Liz?" he asked, smiling. "How what we have just can't disappear overnight?"

The friendship won't disappear, I thought, but the rest of it already has…although I didn't want to keep arguing so I told him to go to work and then I got ready to take my day and a half trip, because I had to and because that was where the new road led.

I was planning to close Samovar down for a mini-vacation while I was gone and not keep dumping on Gemma, but she offered to take over because she needed a new cello and evidently quality instruments ran close to a grand. When she saw Mike waiting outside she smiled.

"It's no big deal…we're just driving to Michigan to investigate something. Off on a *caper*. He's still devastated over you," I said.

She poured boiling water into a pot of Formosa Oolong, which was her favorite and which with her delicate strength she definitely resembled, and we peered down into what's called the agony of the leaves—the swirling rush of heat and water against the loose tea to bring out the most potent brew.

"He would flirt with me but he always watched you," she noted, brushing a wisp of fair hair away from her face. "Like a hawk. Even when his back was turned and you were talking to people at the tables, he'd watch from that mirror over the register. I saw him and I knew who he was really focusing on."

"It's no big deal," I stressed again, and when I wrote out her paycheck I added a hundred dollar bonus for all her extra effort. I could afford a little generosity because even though Samovar was showing just a minor profit, my mother's paintings had been picked up by a calendar company and that had brought in an unexpected extra sum. I've always felt money is karmic and if you get a windfall, you should pass it on. Gemma flushed and thanked me and wished me a fun trip. I took a Chai for the drive and went to the car, which was not a playboy's two-seater like I'd expected but a red SUV, which Mike claimed was better for road trips like this and hauling stuff around.

And we were off. I was somewhat lackluster until we got out of the city, thinking about the talk with David earlier and how screwed up all that was, while Mike was listening to a baseball game on the radio with such rapt attention that it was even more depressing. Who was I kidding, thinking I could have a relationship with this person? I could be a dog in the passenger seat and it wouldn't make much of a difference. I stared out the window at the fleet of trucks alongside us and the industrial plains of northern Indiana that soon became more open and rural.

"You're distant," Mike finally observed when the game had ended.

"You were listening to the radio," I said. "I didn't want to compete."

"I was listening because you were distant," he returned coolly, but then he took my hand. "Sorry. I just figured you had thinking to do, I don't know. You had a far away expression. But then again you've been through a hell of a lot lately and here we are going to see your father."

"Maybe he's my father," I reminded. "Nobody knows for sure."

"Well, if he's not then it's fine…we're just hitting the road. Whatever." He smiled before turning his profile forward again to the highway and I felt myself lighten up. Mike looked like he had gotten a haircut for this adventure. Flat on the sides, a little long on top.

"Take a picture, it'll last longer," he suggested.

"But would it do you justice?" I asked.

He laughed. "Maybe if it was out of focus." The air smelled like fresh cut hay and grass and I had opened my window to breathe it in. "You have something against air conditioning?"

"I do when the air smells like this," I said.

"Okay, but if we start smelling any pig crap then that window goes right back up," he asserted. "Are we driving straight there or should we stop first?"

Stop, I thought. Does he mean stop to have sex or stop to eat or stop to reflect on the entire mission? I couldn't tell. He had sunglasses on once more so I couldn't read his eyes and he hadn't made a single move toward me.

"I don't know," I said nervously. "I'm not sure."

He didn't answer but I saw how behind the glasses his gaze flicked over to me and I realized that he might be unsure and nervous too. He did take the initiative to stop when we got to Michigan, after gassing up at a rest station. He drove a little further to a park area with picnic tables and families scattered here and there, eased into an isolated spot under a large sprawling tree and undid his seatbelt so that he could kiss me.

"It'll be all right," he whispered, his tongue teasing the rim of my ear. "Everything. You and me; seeing your father. Don't get stressed."

And then he kept going further, moving his hands up my skirt, unhooking my bra, kissing my throat and breasts—which was great, I had no problem with any of it, but just not there. I could hear a beagle howling and Styx on a radio somewhere and the seatbelt buckle was digging into my ass. I explained this to Mike who said he couldn't hear anything or anyone, he was honing in exclusively on us and I should do the same.

I pushed back again. "Can we go someplace more private? Just a room with a bed and a roof and a door…it doesn't have to be a palace."

"You really like putting this off," he laughed, re-starting the engine. "Every single time I've started with you you've stopped me. If it ever happens I'll probably explode."

"Maybe it'll be anti-climactic," I said worriedly. "After such build-up."

"As long as it's climactic," he zinged back. "That's enough."

"Maybe that's all you'll want," I babbled on. "Sex. And once you get it you'll take off."

"Once I get it I'll want more sex," he advised. "That's generally how I am. Especially when I find someone who wants to have it but isn't a moron. It's what you call a daily double."

"I'm sorry I couldn't do it in the park," I continued. There were an awful lot of motel signs passing and I knew he was going to veer off toward one at any minute, so I had slipped into constant chatter mode to make it seem less like WE ARE NOW DRIVING TOWARD INTERCOURSE. "I'm a Libra…setting is important to me. God, Mike—what zodiac sign are you? I can't believe I don't know that. Wait, let me guess: Leo."

"No."

"Aries."

"No."

"Scorpio."

"Definitely no—those people are freaks."

"When's your birthday?"

"April 9th."

"But I asked you if you were Aries and you said no," I complained.

"I thought you said Aquarius...I can't hear you with this damn wind blowing through the car."

We ended up at a Motel 6 and I have never seen anyone check in and get keys faster than Mike. The room was clean, beige, forgettable. Heavy-weave burlap draperies blocked out the daylight.

"You're sure you want to do this now?" he said. "Because I can handle it if you don't, just no more stopping and starting. Is this setting okay?"

"It'll do," I said, sitting on one of the beds, which squeaked but was unusually firm and resilient.

"All right then," he replied, easing down next to me and moving into one of his trademark long turn you inside out kisses, yet after a few moments he stopped.

"What's that for?" I asked, trying to catch my breath. "Payback?"

"I don't know." He scowled at the room and flicked his fingers irritably against the polyester bedspread. "This isn't the most exciting place. Maybe we should find something better for the first time. Even doing it outdoors would've been better."

I had brought a few votives and a packet of Gonesh No. 6 incense—they had been in my wedding suitcase and I had figured what the hey, I'm not using them for elopement anymore. I set the candles on the pressed wood bureau, lit a cone of incense and asked if that was better. Mike smiled, glancing around.

"You know, it is," he said. "Much better. What else is in your bag of tricks? Any wine or champagne? Feathers? Handcuffs?"

"I do have a bottle of massage oil," I offered. "Neroli and ylang ylang."

"Okay, that sounds like voodoo juice but pour it on," he urged. "My left shoulder's all cramped from driving. And tension."

He took off his shirt and for the first time since we'd met I looked him over slowly, without any guilt. That was a heady feeling—even an aphrodisiac. I've never really been a person who gets off on guilty pleasures.

"Why are you so tense?" I asked, motioning for him to lie face down so I could work the knots out.

"Because of us," he said, his head at an angle against the pillow. "Not knowing what's going on. What will be going on. Whatever. That feels good, though. That's exactly the spot."

I kneaded the shoulder a little longer then moved my fingers down his ribs to his spine. Then I went from each notch of the spine to just beneath the beltline and reached forward to his hips. He had his eyes closed.

"Are you falling asleep?" I asked.

"I don't think so," he said, then he turned around and pulled me in and that was the end of waiting. He had my clothes and his clothes off as fast as he had gotten the room keys and he went straight to it, almost like we had been having prolonged foreplay every other time. I was ready too, but for just an instant I thought about David and how I hadn't been with anyone else in years and how Mike's body felt harder and rougher. I was almost not going to enjoy the experience because of those thoughts, but then I turned toward the bureau mirror and saw him in action and how incredible that body looked amid the flickering candles (if you edited out the stupid Playboy tattoo) and how it was coming my way and there was no reason he had to stop. After that he had me—and he was considerate too—he slowed down and I could feel him shaking trying to wait until he knew I had finished, then he let loose again. When he was done he was gentle and tender, though there had been a point a few seconds before when I thought he was going to rip me in half from so much pounding.

He rearranged pillows, slid his arm around my waist and collapsed. I was staring at the ceiling, my heart still racing and my body warm and tingling.

"What's wrong?" he asked then, peering at me in the half-light. "Did you fake it? Because I hate that…it drives me nuts."

"I don't fake," I said.

"Then what's the problem? Why are you so serious? What's with the big eyes?"

"I just look serious," I assured him. "I was born like that. With big eyes."

"I know," he said. "I love your eyes. They're like the beginning and the end of the world. Now blow out those candles so we can take a nap and not die in a fire."

I snuffed out the flames and burrowed back in by his side. I wasn't tired and couldn't stop feeling all the long muscles and power to him.

"Was it worth the wait?" I whispered, even though he was falling asleep.

"Almost," he mumbled. "But I'm a really impatient person, I hate waiting for anything. Thirty seconds at a traffic light is too long for me."

I smoothed back his hair and the edge of his sideburn. "Will you want to do it again soon?" I asked.

"Sure, but give me time to reload, Hot Pants. I don't have the same equipment as you." He laughed wearily. "Now *you* have to wait," he said, reaching down to stroke the inner curve of my thigh, while I lay back and tried to control myself—for at least another half hour.

The rest of the afternoon and evening were essentially replays of that episode, only in varying positions and once in the shower. Vague plans were made to go get something to eat but that bed was like quicksand—the more you tried to escape it, the more it pulled you back in. So we ordered from a local Chinese restaurant and shared very sweet pineapple chicken and very bland sesame beef, then we also shared the single fortune cookie which read *Love is standing at your doorstep*. Mike went and checked the doorstep, however, and found only a crumpled package of Camels, which we both agreed did not look much like love.

"Do you think we're in love?" he asked, coming back to the bed after gathering empty take-out containers and throwing them in the trash.

"It could be," I said. "I've seen signs that make me feel I might love you."

"When I gave you the opal?" he prompted, touching it almost possessively.

"No," I said. "The opal is beautiful but it's more like when you wanted to call and point out how Serpico drank tea in the movie. And you couldn't, so it really bothered you. That's the kind of thing that makes me fall in love."

He turned over on his side, watching me intently. "How did you know about the tea in the movie?" he asked. "Did Joe mention it?"

"Yes," I said, realizing that this might be a good time to tell him more about Joe and trying not to let the intent gaze bother me.

"When?"

"At your parents' house. You were passed out on the bed and Joe and I had been talking in the bathroom."

"In the bathroom?" he repeated. "What the hell about? Why would you be alone with Joe in a bathroom away from everybody else?"

I could see he was becoming suspicious, which was quite the wrong detour of thought, so I figured it was now or never. I outlined everything in a calm but detailed manner, gave a brief history of facts, watched Mike now staring like I had grown a third eye.

"Wait," he said, sitting up and shaking his head. "My brother is gay, this is Item Number 1, then my brother was screwing around with *David*, that's Item

Number 2, and then this whole deal with Veronique or whatever her name is is fake, but you and my brother are still big friends and you offered to tell me that he's queer."

"I know it's a lot to absorb, Mike, but—"

"It sounds bogus," he snapped. "It's too contrived."

"Why would anybody make this up?" I laughed in disbelief. "Especially me…you think it's easy to find out that your fiancé was with another man? And not only that, it's a guy you like and you really like his brother? Talk about your head-trips. And imagine learning about it while you're at a party at the other guy's parents' *house*. I mean, I guess it's better than finding them together in a hot tub but—"

"All right, stop, I don't want to think about this shit." Mike put his hands over his face, then sprang up and grabbed his shirt and pants. He dressed quickly, barely looking at me and when he did I saw that his eyes were teary. "I gotta get out of here," he muttered. "This room is like a crazy house. I'll be right back."

An hour passed. Then another, and another, and then I started to contemplate several things. Mike was on his own in a bad way, having taken in some upsetting news, and I began to worry that he'd been in an accident or gotten arrested for mouthing off to a state trooper; or maybe he'd decided to drive back to Chicago to confront Joe, forgetting that I was left without a car in a motel in Nowhere, Michigan—and how could he? Was he like that; did he just always think about himself and his own emotions? By midnight I was still caught between concern and anger and called Joe, but Joe said he hadn't heard from or seen Mike yet. He added that he'd told his mother and even though she'd been upset and had gone to bed with a heartache over unborn grandchildren, he thought she would be able to handle it from now on.

"Mike'll be back," he promised uncertainly. "He's just driving, I'll bet. He likes to drive…he must have just taken off and kept going but he'll turn around soon enough."

At two a.m. I took a portable tea kit Pete had given me with a coil immersion heater and a strainer and cup and fixed some Valerian Dreams. I hoped that would numb my nerves, but it just made me depressive so that I felt even more lost and abandoned. I took another shower, staring at the robin's egg blue speckled tile and recalling how earlier Mike had pressed me against it and pushed himself into me…and then I started thinking about Gemma brewing her tea and how we had watched the hot water and the agony of the leaves. That was what I was going through now, the agony of my leaves. Everything I seemed to have been going through since I'd met Mike was so heightened and extreme, but maybe it was making me stronger and more alive. Maybe. People were like teabags, as Mike himself had quoted. You never knew what was in them until you put them in hot water and made them writhe around.

I dozed off while reading a brochure on Fun Things To Do in Kalamazoo because there was nothing on t.v. and I didn't like focusing on the sound of another couple banging away in the next room along with the rush of traffic on the highway. Wild thunderstorms were passing through and I kept hearing ambulance sirens and imagining horrible crashes or cars skidding off the road into trees. When I woke it was morning and I almost didn't remember where I was or why I was there, but then I saw the candles on the bureau and the Chinese restaurant bag. I felt a pleasant ache in my body and a sharp ache in my heart and it all came back to me. I also saw the fortune cookie slip on the nightstand and focused on it dimly. *Love is standing at your doorstep. Love is standing at your doorstep.*

I got up automatically, like I was sleepwalking, opened the door and saw Mike's SUV right in the parking lot space outside, with Mike slumped behind the wheel. I was angry for perhaps another minute or so, but then I told him to come in and he leaned on me heavily and let me guide him to the bed. He looked drained and worn out like when he'd had his major hangover the other day, but somehow now it was even worse.

"I was driving for about an hour," he explained. "Then I stopped. But I couldn't talk about it yet…I didn't want to talk but I wanted to be close by. I'm sorry. I just don't know how to handle these things."

I told him to get some rest and lay down with him, since I hadn't slept well either. There didn't seem any reason to talk about anything then. It seemed like we had both been through enough.

CHAPTER 11

❀

We kept the room for another day and slept for the better part of it, until about four when Mike asked if I still wanted to keep going to Ann Arbor. I did, but I had been thinking about renting a car and just sneaking in and out of the restaurant on my own while he stayed here. I thought he might want some alone or down time and that it might be best for me to be as unobtrusive as possible around my potential father.

"How about I drive you," Mike offered. "But then I'll wait in the car. I'm not much into being around other people right now."

He hadn't shaved and still looked fairly out of it, sad and disoriented. I almost lost my temper at one point, because he was acting like his brother was dead or dying or had done something awful when all it was was a matter of sexual orientation. Joe didn't have a brain tumor and he hadn't killed anyone. And the only reason he had kept quiet for so long was because he knew there'd be a reaction like this. I nearly told Mike to stop being a Neanderthal and enter the 21st century but then I remembered how even David, one of the most progressive thinkers I knew, was having trouble with the issue. Not wanting to be perceived as gay, not wanting to be *like that*. So I backed off from Mike and concentrated on the next dip coming on the Tilt a Whirl: Mr. Gilberto Fonseca.

Ann Arbor was a pretty college town, maybe a shade less populated than usual because it was summer session but still fairly busy and diverse. The Fado place Gilberto Fonseca owned was a few miles further away in Ypsilanti, which I had never thought much about beyond its being one of those rare cities that began with a Y to use when you were playing Geography. Fado, which I had learned meant a name for a particular kind of ballad in Portugal, was a nice grotto type place, with candles at every table and wine colored drapes and linens. Mike gave me a good luck kiss and I went and sat at the bar, which was mahogany and intricately carved with twisting leaf patterns. The restaurant was beginning to fill up and looked like *the* local spot to take first dates or propose or celebrate anniversaries—you just felt a pulse of magic and warmth in the air as soon as you came in. I scanned the room in a restrained panic for Gilberto Fonseca but he didn't seem to be around; the bartender asked if I wanted anything so I ordered a glass of Mateus and tried not to gulp it all at once.

"Are you waiting for someone?" the bartender kept on, smiling pleasantly. He was cute—I hadn't noticed at first because he wasn't exactly my type—he was more alternative than I usually cared for, with a shaved head and a Vandyke beard. But his eyes were velvety brown and he made smooth, easygoing motions as he served drinks or picked up tips. I said I was supposed to meet my boyfriend and left it at that. My plan was to see Gilberto play, hold back the tears, then leave in a shroud of mystery. But Gilberto hadn't taken the stage yet, even though it was past six o'clock. When I'd called earlier they had noted that he played from six through nine each night, but it was six-thirty now and music was floating from a hidden sound system with no sign of live entertainment in the works. He's probably sick or has a toothache or carpal tunnel syndrome, I thought disgustedly. The one night I show up he'll be elsewhere.

The bartender then asked if I was local or visiting from someplace. I told him Chicago, after a moment. A lot of people lived in Chicago.

"That's a cool city," he said. "I try to get down there every couple of months. Just for a change of pace. Ann Arbor gets a little bo-ring sometimes."

He poured out a Brandy Alexander for the waitress then set a tin of clove cigarettes on the bar. "Almost break time," he noted.

"I love clove cigarettes," I said, because I did even though I could only finish about half of one before I got too dizzy.

"Help yourself." He extended the pack and I took one while he lit it. I took a shaky first puff, then got more into it and all the fragrant smoke drifting around. And then from nowhere, Gilberto Fonseca stepped onto a small platform and began to play and I almost dropped hot ash onto my bare knee.

Okay, there he is, I thought. Hold it together…he's just one of the many men who slept with your mother and a couple of chromosomes connected. But he was such a laidback man with a brilliant talent, so skilled with the guitar and naturally connecting with his audience. He wasn't big, maybe five-seven, a hundred and forty pounds tops, his hair was thinning like Mike and I had noticed on-line and his face not exactly remarkable, but there was a subtle magnetism, especially around the eyes. And in the gestures and the quiet smile. I stifled something between a laugh and a sob and kept watching, even though he had paused to tighten and tune guitar strings while talking to one of the waiters. And then I felt an arm around my waist—it was Mike, who had found a suit jacket somewhere and snuck in.

"How long have you been here?" I almost shrieked, because he had completely startled me—I thought it was some drunk or a man who'd mistaken my back view for another female form.

"Ten, fifteen minutes." He nodded to the bartender, who was going to take his own clove cigarette break. "You were chatting with your buddy, I didn't want to interrupt. But I did want to watch your reaction when your Dad came out. And besides, I could smell the onions and the seafood from the kitchen back door when I was in the parking lot. Can we eat here, please? I'm starving."

"Oh, Mike…I don't know if I can get through a meal, watching him," I whispered, nodding to Gilberto Fonseca, now back to playing again. Mike took my cigarette and put it out before I let the glowing tip burn off my fingers.

"Let's give it a try," he urged. "Seriously. You can't come all this way just to rush in and out."

I listened to the music and knew I wasn't going anywhere. Although when the headwaiter showed us to the table right in front of Gilberto Fonseca, I balked.

"No! Can't we sit there?" I asked, pointing to a dim-lit corner nook.

"She's in the Witness Protection Program…she likes being incognito," Mike joked, easing us both over to the shadows before we drew any more attention.

Mike ordered food and it was put in front of me and I remember liking the taste of it—rice with rosemary, pork with red peppers and lemon, a seafood stew and thank God more pale fruity wine—but I couldn't focus on the names of the dishes or much else about them. But by the time we had dessert and coffee (I needed the strong kick of coffee even though I was pleased to see three kinds of tea, or chá on the menu) I had relaxed into the same melancholy sweetness that I'd felt when I was playing the Gilberto and Gilberto record in the dark. Mike on the other hand was finishing my dessert and his own.

"These people don't screw around," he praised, easing his fork through a flower-like fig stuffed with almond and chocolate and whipped cream. "Their food is almost as good as Italian cooking. *Almost.* But then Italian food is the best in the world, so it's hard to beat."

He winked and gave me a taste. It was another of those moments with Mike when you were amazed by his charm and how happy he made you feel, even during an uneasy situation. And how he looked so charmingly seedy in his rumpled suit jacket with the day's growth of beard. I reached out and held the hand that wasn't busy with the fork and we sat like that, quietly, but then I got distracted again. Gilberto Fonseca was staring and had turned toward us with the guitar while he was playing. And he stared and stared. I felt like I was on fire, or like I had the hugest most glaring spotlight in the world beamed on me full force. Soon I couldn't stand it and hurried to the ladies' room, where a woman was expertly pumping her breasts and putting the milk into a container for later. She smiled when I came in.

"Do you have any kids?" she asked. I was still flustered but I mumbled no, I did not.

"I think I'm going to bottle feed the next one," she sighed. "I really miss a good glass of red wine at dinner. Especially at Fado. Boy, I love this restaurant and the wonderful music he plays."

I blundered into a stall and tried to regain composure. No major crisis, I thought, he just turned toward you because you were with Mike and he figures you're either deeply in love or on a first date. And that's completely fine because you are more or less on a first date with Mike, since you've never done anything formal or in public with him. So go back out to the table and look loving and simply smile at the man who you want to pounce on and hug and scream *Please say you're my FATHER!*

So that's what I went to do, after taking as much time as possible to reapply lipstick and to practice getting that abandoned war orphan look out of my eyes. When I approached the table, however, Gilberto Fonseca was sitting across from Mike. I almost ran out the door, but Mike knew me well enough to jump up and catch me by the arm.

"Listen," Mike began. "He knows. I told him."

"How could you?" I demanded and I thought I was going to faint, I was so upset yet so overwhelmed by having this man right next to me and now taking my other arm.

"We'll go into my office and talk for a little while," Gilberto said, firmly leading me to some back door beyond the bar and a bunch of plants. Another guitar player had taken over and some couple was popping Dom Perignon to celebrate twenty-five years of happiness so the three of us managed to slip away without being noticed. I sat in a chair in the office and tried not to look at family portraits on his desk or any personal effects. Or even him, particularly. But he continued to stare at me.

"I don't want you to be angry with your boyfriend, Liz," he insisted. "Please." He had a rich, lyrical voice, almost like an actor or a preacher—someone who really knew how to use the power of the spoken word. Only a slight accent. But then according to the article I had read on the Internet he had been in this country almost three decades. Practically my entire lifespan.

"When you left the table I thought you might be upset or not feeling well, so I asked Mike what was wrong," he continued. "I said that I was sorry to have stared, but you look exactly like my mother did when she was a young woman. So then he felt that he had to tell me why you were really here."

"Oh God," I said, starting to cry. Gilberto Fonseca smiled and offered a box of tissues. "Do you remember my mother?" I burst out. "Did you even know her that well?"

His smile became tighter and somewhat embarrassed. "Yes, I knew her," he said. "We were...together for a while. She wanted to make my friend Gilberto—you know, the guy I used to sing with—jealous so she came after me. The other Gilberto was crazy about her friend, who was also a model but she was from England. Or maybe Finland...something with a *land* at the end of it. I guess it doesn't matter. I was flattered to be with your mother and we took a trip to Madeira together, but then she suddenly decided she'd had enough of Portugal and she wanted to go on to Spain. Alone. She tended to change her mind every hour then. Sometimes every half hour." He sighed heavily. "I can't believe she's gone. That Bethy died...she had such energy and spirit."

"I know," I said. "She was something else."

A clock ticked on the wall and chimed eight times. Gilberto Fonseca folded his hands and resumed talking.

"So it is likely that you're my daughter," he said. "And I think that's incredible, to see you here looking so much like my own mother, who I always thought was the loveliest woman in the world. But my wife," he added, motioning to one of the framed photos on his desk, a dark woman with a pixie cut and delicate features. "Isn't fond of anything I did before I met her. Anything relating to my more liberated past." He laughed morosely. "I would love to see you all the time but I can't, my wife just won't take it well. I came to Ann Arbor because of her, she teaches Portuguese Literature at the University. We have a daughter and two sons of our own—the boys work here in the restaurant. Marco is playing the guitar now and Benny is the bartender."

"The bartender?" Mike repeated, and I saw him smirk a bit because he knew and I knew that I had been attracted to and flirting with my own half-brother. I felt a creepy shudder go up and down my spine. Damn Bethy and her *spirit*.

"Tell me what you do now," Gilberto insisted. "Mike mentioned a tearoom. You're an enterprising soul too, I suspect."

I strung together some disjointed details and handed him one of my Samovar business cards. He smiled at the tea-colored paper.

"Here's a little history about your heritage," he said. "The Portuguese were the first Europeans to drink tea in China and to bring it back home. And it was evidently because of Catherine of Braganza, a Portuguese princess who married Charles the Second of England, that the British even took up the custom of afternoon tea. So it's in your blood, I'd say. What do you think of that?"

Mike applauded and laughed but I wanted to cry again, because here I was finally meeting my intelligent, talented, enterprising and steady as a rock father and I couldn't make up for lost time or even have him in my future. He seemed to pick up on the longing and pocketed my business card.

"Let me think about this," he said. "I don't know that I can let you just drift away again. I'll have to figure something out."

Then he stood up and we stood up and he told us that our check had been taken care of and if we wanted to stay for more drinks we were welcome to, but I looked glumly at Mike and he said no, we really had to go. My father shook Mike's hand and kissed me on both cheeks, then held me briefly while I almost wished that all my bones could melt into his and we could start over again. He went back to his guests and we left super-casually, passing Benny at the bar who called to me that I should come again whenever I was in town.

"Watch it, Benny, you're playing with a loaded gun," Mike quipped, and even though I told him to shut up or die I was still glad to have Mike around, for comic and otherwise relief.

The otherwise relief from Mike was explosive and insane, following the drive home. We rode in fairly mellow quiet, with me psychologically digesting and Mike digesting the better part of two dinners he'd polished off, and by the time we were almost back to the motel I had decided not to let this thing with Gilberto get hurtful—that the flow of the Universe had brought him to me at a specific point in time and would keep him around somehow, but I shouldn't obsess.

And since I had established harmony within myself once more, it was time for another emotional tidal wave, which happened when Mike stopped for gas.

It was hot and some nymphet was at the next pump wearing a crocheted halter with more holes than yarn and cutoffs so low in the waist that you could see her crack, and of course Mike looked. He looked and he smiled, and I had the most vicious urge to start the engine, run him down then go into reverse until he was pulp. I had never felt such rage over a look and a smile—there had been times that David would flirt or banter with salesgirls or perhaps even salesmen, I just hadn't thought to question that whole deal and figured he was just being friendly. But I had never lost my temper or even called him on it, because I had always felt that in minor forms that was natural and part of being male or female. Now, however, I was livid. I wanted to kill Mike *and* Lolita, then use her slutty top to tie them together at the necks like two dead turkeys.

"What's wrong?" he said when he got back behind the wheel. I knew I was glaring—I could see my face in the reflection of the passenger window and it didn't look like me at all. The woman in the window was an excited, fierce person with enormous eyes and reminded me of someone from a foreign movie with a lot of sweaty, heaving sex scenes, but she wasn't me.

"Don't flirt when I'm fucking sitting right here and can see you!" I retorted, or rather the foreign actress persona retorted, while Mike stared in complete surprise. But then I watched a shadowy grin cross his face. He secretly likes this, I thought. He's riding that big green wave of jealousy with pleasure.

"I just smiled," he laughed. "Don't be crazy. She's trying to get attention and I wanted to let her know she's doing a good job."

"I always knew that was your real type," I scoffed. "The Skank."

"She's not exactly a skank and she'd be lots of guys' type," he advised, turning back onto the highway. "Men tend to go for the obvious. You put it in the window, they'll stop and look."

"So you do like skanks," I decided.

"I said on a *surface* level…Jesus!" he yelled, flooring it past a rickety pickup full of scrap metal and furniture that looked like it belonged to Fred G. Sanford. "And that's all I did was look! I didn't take a cigarette from her or laugh at every stupid thing she said. But then again, she wasn't my half-sister so I wasn't that turned on. And by the way, I hope you don't smoke on a regular basis because I don't like chicks who do."

"Okay, first of all, drop the incest business right *now* because it wasn't funny to begin with. And secondly, I don't like guys who call women *chicks*," I snapped. "And thirdly, I'll smoke a freaking pack a day if it's what I want."

"No, you won't!" he threatened. "I hate goddamn smokers."

"Shut up," I muttered. He complained that he was sick of me telling him to shut up, so I told him again. For lack of anything else, he grabbed a vial of Tic-Tacs from the dashboard and threw it at my head. I took the blow, but then reached over to punch his arm and I mean I punched hard, knuckles to bone. I wasn't fooling around.

"All right, that's enough," he said tersely. "I'm driving, don't mess with me…I don't want to crash."

When we reached the motel a few minutes later he lurched into the first available spot and I jumped out before the engine had even died, heading for our door. I had the perverse urge to get away but I also really, really wanted him to follow. He followed, of course, because he had the room key, and while he maneuvered it into the lock I then had another perverse urge to slide my hands down his pants. What the hell am I doing, I thought. He's going to turn around, pick me up and hurl me into the next county.

"You're completely mental," he announced, forcing the door open with his knee since it tended to stick, but I could feel heat coming off him and I kept at it. We stood very close in the darkened room and you could almost see a current like static electricity flickering between us, and then we just went insane. We had each been through such a haul over the past few days that we seemed to have to let it all go; it seemed like therapy to tear and bite and slam into the closest anchoring surface. I don't remember the end too well because I truly blacked out for about thirty seconds. When I woke I was lying with my head tipped back against the edge of the mattress and could feel his heart thudding against my own but I couldn't tell the beats apart. I had never had sex like that in my life. I felt like the sky after a Fourth of July blitzkrieg finale of fireworks.

"That was great," Mike said when he could breathe, and then he helped me back onto the full expanse of the bed and not just its most strategic leverage angle. "We have chemistry."

That was berserk, I thought, for some reason remembering old 1970s tabloids of Elizabeth Taylor and Richard Burton and how I would always see them at my grandmother's house as a child. Their relationship had seemed so volatile that it had never made sense to me, but now I perhaps understood a bit more of what had kept them together. Just a bit, I thought, amazed to feel that the opal on its delicate chain had survived and was still in place around my neck, whereas everything else had been torn off and was scattered around the room.

I never did find my bra.

CHAPTER 12

❀

Back in Chicago Mike and I parted ways briefly to deal with our latest hand of cards, as he put it—for him the situation with his brother, for me whatever was happening with David. Mike looked grim as he said goodbye but I had a feeling that once he saw Joe and spoke to him again, the confusion and the differences would lessen and they would go on like they had before. Not exactly as they'd been, of course, but when brothers were close, it was almost impossible to pull them apart. Meanwhile David had not moved his furniture and belongings out and had only left an upset, even outraged phone message for me about knowing who I'd gone away with, that it was "indiscriminate" and that I should be aware that it disgusted him.

"But being involved with his brother isn't disgusting, that's just you being *complex*," I said, deleting the message, but then I felt the urge to confront him in person and rip right back into his lawyerly rhetoric. He had noted that he'd be working late if I cared to rebut, so I took the train downtown to his firm and sailed past the receptionist, who still seemed to think David and I were engaged. Which was a logical conclusion, since David still had pictures of me on his desk and bookshelf and put up a big love-fest front when I came in. I ignored the two other attorneys he was talking to and went to his office; he joined me within a few minutes and closed the door.

"Don't ever leave messages like that again," I warned. "You have no right."

"I don't, but I was hoping that after five years you could wait maybe a *week*," he shot back. "And that you might have more class in your choice of partners."

"You liked his brother enough," I reminded.

"His brother is different," David said, and for an instant I saw something cross his face that made me think he might really care about Joe. "His brother is on a whole other plane of existence. He's not so obvious and…whatever."

"You don't know Mike so don't call him obvious. And you must have talked to Joe to find out where I was," I guessed, but David just snatched up a tissue to wipe his glasses and glared at his telephone, which wouldn't stop ringing. To be honest, even though I didn't want to notice or care too much, David looked worn to the bone. He had stacks of files everywhere and appeared to be in the middle of some big case preparation. I asked what was going on.

"What else…major patent infringement bullshit," he sighed. "I tell you, I'm seriously starting to hate lawyers."

I smiled, despite the argument we were taking a sidebar on. There's a crude saying that if you want to get over one man you should get under another, but it hadn't quite put enough distance between David and me and I still couldn't help looking at him with affection and wanting our old life back. But then I looked at him more closely along with the framed pictures he had of either me or the two of us together, and I began to wonder how much of our old life had been real and how much had been for display.

"Liz, please," he then urged, motioning to the chaos around him. "I'm falling apart without you. Let's forget whatever happened with Mike and Joe and call it even. We can get counseling together, we can start over but all the secrets will be out. It's almost like this had to happen in order for us to have the great marriage we were meant to enjoy. We can go through anything together after this."

As I listened I realized that he made some sense and that even though he'd been trained to be professionally persuasive, he meant what he said. And that even with the betrayal or whatever it should be called, there was enough to carry us through and I still felt so calm in his presence. Like we were meant to be, I had felt that way from the minute I'd met him. But then I thought of Mike throwing Tic-Tacs at me in the car and I laughed. I thought of Mike shaking hands with my father and Mike telling me my eyes were the beginning and the end of the world, and how just that morning Mike had picked a bunch of pale purple lilacs and left them with a twenty dollar bill in the motel cleaning lady's cart, because she was older and huffing along and because he had had to clean motel rooms himself once and it was usually lousy work.

"It's not all sex," I suddenly said, laughing again. "There's a lot more."

I had meant with Mike, of course, but David misunderstood me.

"There is much more," he agreed, hunching forward. "And this is why we can do it. Not that we ever had a sexual problem…I just—"

"No," I said, getting up. "Don't. Don't talk about it now; I can't go through that. You should get some counseling on your own and you should even get out of this place before it sucks the soul out of you. David, go back to that point where you were standing in front of the antique store in college," I insisted, thinking about my framed picture of him. "That's who you are. You and your eyes behind the glasses," I added incoherently, because I was on the verge of losing it. "Your incredible gray eyes with the green ring around the pupils. Those are the real eyes most people never see."

I almost tripped over a file in my race to get out of there; I was racing because he was coming after me and I was afraid if he caught me I wouldn't be able to break away. David was an intellectual property attorney and there were prototypes for toys here and there—jumping pigs, robot parrots—which made it like running through a surreal funhouse. In the hall I turned left instead of heading for the elevator bank like he would have expected, then I ran down twenty-two flights of zigzagging fire stairs until there were no more stairs left and I did not see those wide and perfectly-spaced eyes anymore, a gray as clear as ice with just the finest rim of green.

When I went to Samovar the next morning there was a bizarre surprise waiting: streams of water flowing from the two cherrywood ceiling fans. The heavy thunderstorms that had been in Michigan the other night had circled back through Chicago around dawn and caused all kinds of damage: fallen tree branches, battered petunias, power outages and flash floods. Evidently the roof had been hit with too much rain at once and the weight had caused leakages, particularly at the center of the roof, which connected to the ceiling, which connected to the fans. I only had the fans on for a minute until I realized that I was either hallucinating or there were some serious waterworks spiraling downward from the blades.

Fortunately the damage was mostly in the ceiling and one section of the back wall—I say fortunately because I didn't own the building but I did own the tables and chairs of the tearoom along with the tablecloths, tapestries and samovars, the antique cash register, and so on. My mother's paintings hadn't been ruined either; somehow her *Splendiforous Camellia* had been hanging on the wall that was most affected but the water seemed to have spread around it. I could just imagine telling her agent that the flower had drowned. He was already enough of a pony-tailed snit as it was, and he still couldn't stand the fact that I had her greatest last canvases hanging in some *Ravenswood* (Ravenswood was so incredibly *sleepy* as he always sneered) *tearoom* without any reference to his gallery and that I refused to sell them to anyone and give him his fifteen percent commission.

At any rate, I couldn't open for customers that morning and instead got busy calling my landlord who called an electrician, then I mopped the floor and brought some damp tablecloths to the laundry. The electrician was from Dublin and while he worked went on about how he wouldn't drink tea with "spices and candy" (like Chai or Vanilla Hazelnut) and that real tea should be black as night and strong as an ox. I filled his thermos with Irish Breakfast after letting it steep forever so it would take the enamel off his teeth and he'd be happy. Some other man clomped around the roof and cleared away any remaining standing water while I scraped off the paint that had blistered on the south wall. I was trying to make the wall itself ready to be repainted faster by hitting the wet patches with a blow dryer when Mike banged on the door and I hurried to let him in, smiling. He didn't smile back, however.

"What are you doing here?" he yelled, gesturing around. "Why didn't you come get me right away?"

I looked at him blankly then shook my head. "I don't know…it didn't occur to me to come get you. It's not like the furniture was floating around or the ceiling had caved in."

"You should have called me regardless," Mike said, peevishly inspecting the wall and a few snips of discarded wire on the ground. "I shouldn't have to find stuff like this out from Crazy Mary, who said you were closed."

"I would have told you later," I said, wondering why he was making such a major fuss. "After the mess was cleared up. You have your own business to run, remember?"

"Are you like really prideful?" he persisted. "Do you hate to take help?"

"Mike, what are you talking about?" I laughed. "I just take care of things when I can. That's how I've always been…when I was growing up if I didn't handle something, nobody would. I mean, my mother certainly didn't deal with reality too often."

Ironically I was drinking some iced hibiscus, my mother's old favorite, and I hadn't been able to drink it since she'd passed away without getting misty. But it was fine now and I enjoyed the taste and the memory of her without sadness, and I poured a glass for Mike. He drained it because it was hot outside and he was surely thirsty, but I noticed that he did make a face at the slightly sour tang.

"How's Joe?" I asked. "And you. How are you both?"

"We're okay," he said, back to inspecting the wall. "It was a little tense at first but what can you do. He's still just Joey, I guess. He mentioned that your pal David called him while we were away."

"I know," I said. "David was pretty mad about our trip. He left a nasty voicemail message until I talked to him and straightened things out. I think he was wondering whether you and I were involved before."

I left out the part about David noting that Mike had no class. "He should talk," Mike scoffed. "Here you put me off for months and he's monkeying around with my own brother. But let's not open that big gaping wound again. Not when I finally got the band-aid to stay put."

"Let's not," I agreed. "In fact, when I came in here this morning I was almost glad to see an actual mess I could do something about instead having to handle any more human drama. This is nothing in comparison."

I was just contemplating whether I should give the wood floors a good hand waxing when Mike gripped my elbow.

"Wait, you said David left you a nasty message?" he demanded. "Why didn't you call me about that?"

I shook my head again, back to being confused. "I didn't call because I could handle it. Also, I knew you had your own problems to keep you busy because you were talking to Joe. I'm not trying to freeze you out, Mike, I just don't need you to fight all my battles."

"But you should involve me," he objected. "You should immediately think of connecting with me when something bad or really great happens…or any time you have something to say. That's how I see a partnership. Constant inter-action."

This was why he'd gotten so down about not being able to tell me about the Serpico tea thing, I supposed. He was more of a coupler than I'd thought. David and I had been close but we had also generally gone about our own lives and connected at the end of the day. I realized something then and it made me smile, but in a vaguely nervous way. Mike was a little high maintenance. He was the needing to be needed type. He would probably never let you make a major decision like buying a car or signing a lease without him. And while that certainly would appeal to some women, it felt kind of invasive to me.

But then Mike was wearing a tight white t-shirt and a pair of jeans with just the right fade to the denim and just the right fit, and maybe it wasn't so bad to be invaded. I sat on his lap and started to kiss him, but he stopped me after a few seconds and moved me firmly to my own chair.

"We need to set a course," he said. "I have to know where this is all going before I invest any more time. Let's talk about three month, six month and one year scenarios. First of all, is this marriage oriented?"

"I just got out of a long engagement," I reminded. "I was supposed to elope today. Do I have to decide about another marriage already?"

"You should know by now," he insisted. "These things are intuitive. My father and mother knew they were getting married on the first date. What's your gut feeling?"

"Uh, strong," I said. "But—"

"Don't mix it up with sex, though," he went on. "Go a little higher, to the stomach." He slapped himself in the flat, firm, bounce a quarter off it abdomen. "Right there. What's it telling you about us?"

It seemed amazing that someone so handsome could be so demented. I laughed, but in the same nervous way as when I'd been smiling.

"Haven't you ever heard of going with the flow?" I asked.

"Hell, no," he laughed. "If I did that I'd be married to that chick you met at my parents' party and on the city payroll like my Dad, with three kids and a house in Orland Park. Only half my potential would be fulfilled and I'd just be working to pay a mortgage and bills for shit I didn't really want. Forget the flow. I direct my own destiny."

He's demented but unique, I have to admit that, I thought. He has his own unique demented logic.

"A couple of other things too," he noted, turning the chair around so that he could straddle it and speak with more conviction. "I don't know some vital facts about you, like where did you go to college, who'd you lose your virginity to and at what age, and what's your favorite color. Oh, yeah, and when's your birthday? You already know mine, we talked about it in the car."

I prayed to God or whoever that he wouldn't ask me for the exact date, because I'd been pretty jumpy in the car and could only remember that it was sometime in April.

"Come on," he prodded. "Give me the facts."

I rolled my eyes. "I lost my virginity at age eighteen to a graduate student in college named George. I made a big point of holding onto it and waiting for the best guy because I wanted to do the opposite of what my mother said, which was to sleep with anyone for and jump right into the love pool. I went to Columbia College and got a Bachelor of Fine Arts; I was born on October 20th and my favorite color is red. Well, now it's red…but it used to be blue."

"Great, great," he praised. "That all adds to the picture. I went to St. Xavier College but dropped out to work on the Board of Trade; I lost my virginity to my best friend's sister, who moved to Boston and completely ripped out my heart; you know my birthday and my favorite color is purple. But it used to be red."

To be honest, even though I didn't like the abruptness, he was right in that those swift facts did add a lot to the total picture. Encouraged, he kept going after first glancing at his watch.

"Now let's work out a basic timeframe for our situation…but I only have a few minutes before I have to get back and give Joe a break. What's the plan; when do we talk about living together, engagement, marriage? I don't think we should walk away at this point. There's a definite connection."

"Maybe we should discuss this in more depth," I suggested delicately. "Over a bottle of wine on a Sunday night…or when you have more than two minutes to spare."

"I really need to know now," he persisted. "I don't like gray areas, I never have. Just throw out a general idea. Nothing needs to be carved in stone."

I'd like to take a stone and hit you in the skull with it, I thought, but then I remembered that Mike was an Aries and that's usually how Aries men were. They craved competition, force, and the game of life; they needed goalposts, mile markers, teammates and cheering sections. And even though the thought of being with Mike theoretically until death did us part gave me a combined sensation of excitement, heartburn and the bed spins, I also knew that this might all burn itself out and have the lifespan of a firefly. So I hit the ball back.

"We can talk about living together in one month, engagement in three months and if we're still speaking a year from today, I'll discuss marriage." I laughed. "We could even get married a year from this very minute, depending on how things go…how's that for specific. It was supposed to be my wedding day on some cosmic calendar."

"Fine, that's enough for now," he said, pushing back off the chair and pinching my cheek. "I think you're trying to call my bluff or something but we'll see how you hold up. It would be a big wedding, right?"

"Absolutely not," I replied. "I hate big weddings."

He pursed his lips. "Okay, we'll work that out later."

"When you have another free minute," I agreed. "Maybe while you're brushing your teeth."

He just sort of waved his hand at me and kept walking, yet then he came back.

"When you redo that wall put a couple capfuls of bleach in the paint," he advised. "In case there's still some dampness…it'll stop mold from growing through."

"I thought you wanted to paint it," I said.

"You said you had it under control," he countered. "Should I help? Or should I just do it? I don't mind."

I said that while I appreciated the offer, I would take care of the wall. And that I had originally painted Samovar by myself, after all.

"I know you painted the tearoom because that's when I first met you, while you were working on it. You were up on that ladder like the angel on top of the Christmas tree," Mike said. "Did you want me then?" he teased. "Were you barely able to control yourself?"

"My body wanted you but my mind said no, no, no." I smiled, remembering how much he had unnerved me.

Mike leaned forward. "You should never listen to your mind, Lizzie, not when I'm here to do the thinking for you," he murmured. I reached up to slap him and he grabbed my hand and we ended up having an arm wrestle, only he definitely let me win. Otherwise there'd be no contest—he had so much sinew in his arms that it would be like trying to wrestle a cobra.

"There, you pinned me," he said. "I'm yours. And I am so frigging late…I just told Joe I was taking out the garbage."

He bolted up again, skidding through the last of the water puddled on the floor. "Have fun painting," he called back to me and I said that I would, especially if he brought me a three-nut brownie and an Orangina like he had the first time, and made my energy level spike once more.

CHAPTER 13

❀

Spencer, my mother's agent, called to have lunch soon after the ceiling fan flood, although he never knew how close *Splendiforous Camellia* came to drowning and he never would. I really had an intense dislike for Spencer and his affectations, his ponytail and asexual monotone voice, even though I had tried to remain open-minded and not file him away under Pretentious Gallery Owner. But that's what he was: A Pretentious River North Gallery Owner. Some people just not only fit the stereotype, they're the ones the stereotype was made from. Spencer generally wore snaky green or taupe or gray tones, to match his glittering serpentine eyes. He spoke in the same constant tone of drawling indifference, he smiled only when professionally necessary and when he did smile it was unconvincing, just the slightest stretch of the mouth—more like a grimace. He was somewhere between the ages of forty and seventy and it seemed that at some point he had had all his blood replaced with embalming fluid. I knew the meeting was a schmoozing session to try to make me turn all of Mom's paintings over to him, but since I had no intention of ever doing that I focused more on enjoying the lunch itself.

We met at the Russian Tea Time Café down by the Art Institute on my suggestion; Spencer surely would have preferred a more minimalist place like Zealous or Spring, but I wanted my Russian tea service and the whole red-gold ornate ambience, balalaika music, waiters in white high collared shirts and black trousers bending stiffly from the waist like you were deposed Romanoff royalty.

Spencer focused on the paintings and his agenda for them while I kept turning the conversation back to him, trying to find out where he had come from and whether he had formed from a pod, but the closest verification I could get was that he had been raised in Ohio. He sneered at my entrée, crepes stuffed with meat and onions in an avocado-coriander dressing, while picking at a smoked salmon club and pomegranate sorbet like it was a pile of sawdust. However, I did see him getting a little lustful toward my dessert, which was the Black Russky, three layers of chocolate mousse—dark, milk and white—on a pool of more chocolate. I think that dessert may have penetrated through to the real Spencer, the freaky kinky man who no doubt liked to be tied up and trussed and who secretly hid in closets sucking down Bosco before smearing it all over his hairless white body.

But I was trying to eat, so I stopped that visual accompaniment. I caught Spencer glancing at his watch so I began to chew very slowly, to hold him hostage, and I asked for another glass of tea. I was having Darjeeling Makaibari even though I usually drank Russian Caravan when I came there, but Russian Caravan reminded me too much of David and Joe and it was time for a change. While the waiter was pouring more for me and looking like he longed so for his fur hat and the White Nights of St. Petersburg, a young woman approached our table and spoke to Spencer. Her name was Abigail. Spencer acknowledged her with a two-second grimace and asked her with no sincerity whatsoever to join us.

Abigail was initially another sneering chilly type but I sensed warmth and a heartbeat behind the cool facade and figured she had just become that way to deal with people like Spencer. Evidently, they had connected on some public relations issues in the past as Abigail worked for a boutique P.R. agency. She had super-short hair and wore black cat's eye glasses with white frosted lipstick, something you could only pull off if you were rail thin, which she was, and had a perfect nose, which she did. She was fascinated about the tearoom and my mother and apparently my entire life, and since this was far too much personal information for Spencer to handle, he excused himself after dourly paying the check. Abigail then said she wanted to try a tisane, or a fruit tea, so she ordered Mandarin Chamomile. We started talking about my habit of matching people's personalities with tea, and I told her that she had asked for exactly what I would have typed her as. She looked like she had the sensibility and even temper of chamomile, while the mandarin twist gave her independent thought and style. At this point she removed a pink and black op art notebook from a purple fake croc clutch bag and started to write things down.

"Tell me, would you be interested in hooking up with a charity event?" she asked with a secret sparkle behind the cat's eye frames, like oh, say yes, it'll be too much fun. "Because I do a few things for not for profits every once in a while and we always have a low budget, but that's the most challenging stuff. I'm getting an idea here for you to host a tea at Samovar, only you'd have about six private tables of a special tea with a special person. Do you see what I'm saying?"

I didn't, so I shook my head.

"Okay, hear me out," she continued, brushing her chin with the end of her pen, which was crowned by a green feather. "The place I want to team you with is Animal House, a shelter for cats and dogs on the edge of your neighborhood. It's just an old warehouse that a group of people bought and cleaned out and set up so that abandoned pets and strays could live there. They have a little yard for the cats and a walking area for the dogs…and of course they're no-kill. They do well enough with donations and adoption fees and most vets donate their services for free, but they could always use more cash flow. I think they're trying to put in a central air system so it's not so hot in the summer, and I was thinking if we take their donor base and court it with a promotion of having tea with a beautiful stranger, we could raise a quick grand. And you'd get publicity and exposure. Wouldn't you like that?"

"That's always good," I agreed. "Especially for a worthy cause. But what do you mean by tea with a beautiful stranger?"

She tapped at the list of teas on the menu. "Well, let's take six fairly well-known teas and personify them, like you call it, and come up with six profiles of attractive men or women. Maybe make one or two gay or lesbian, to offer the option…you know, discreetly put down male or female for their preference. Gays and lesbians are big supporters of animal rights and statistics show they tend to own pets."

"But not all of them do," I said cryptically. "Anyhow, go on."

"All right…then you write a profile of each tea dream date and how he or she is like the tea itself, and we offer an hour's sumptuous tea service and conversation with that person for $150. If you do two sessions with six sittings, that's $1,800, minus your overhead. But you can get other businesses to donate their part and get on the roster of sponsors, like pastry shop owners, florists, caterers. You leave that to me. All I need you to do is to write up the profiles and provide the venue. And the teas. Could you do that?"

"I suppose," I said. "But who will the actual people be?"

"Oh, between you and me both we'll supply the bodies," she insisted, fluffing that question away with the feather pen. "Right now I can promise you an Englishman for Earl Grey and a gay Chinese guy for green tea."

"Is the Chinese guy soft-spoken?" I asked hopefully.

"Yes," Abigail said. "But he's also a powerhouse. He has an incredible body…he reminds me of one of those Shaolin monks. The ones who practice Buddhism and kung fu. Why, any ideas?"

"I think Green Lychee," I said. "That's when the leaves are bound together with silk, like a lychee nut, then they open slowly like a flower when you pour hot water on them. See, it's on the menu here too," I noted.

Abigail clutched my wrist. "This is fantastic. To be honest, I like doing the charity things better than the corporate functions. I mean those people are such corpses sometimes, they have no imagination. Or they always have these women who are ex-cheerleaders running their Events Departments and trying to pretend they have half a brain and didn't get their job because they blew somebody. And I'm so glad I met you even though it was through that weasel Spencer Baird." She touched up her frosted lips before the mirror of a jeweled case then crinkled her exquisite nose. "Do you know he goes to leather bars?" she whispered. "Almost every night?"

"Doesn't surprise me in the least," I said, and then we went back to her notebook to work out the remaining five types of tea.

We ended up with Earl Grey, Russian Caravan, Green Lychee, Rose Congou, Bombay Chai and Chocolate Velvet for the teas, and the Russian Caravan was dependent upon whether I could get Joe to participate. I knew he would balk and say he wasn't conversational or exciting enough, but I also knew that whether he wanted to play it straight or gay, he would tempt someone into paying for his teatime. He just had that quiet, cute Clark Kent appeal and was so good-natured and courtly—he'd be a perfect partner. Abigail supplied the men for Earl Grey, Green Lychee and Chocolate Velvet, while I asked Gemma if she would handle Rose Congou (a fragrant tea infused with rose petals). Normally I thought of Gemma as Formosa Oolong, but Rose Congou was more exotic and intriguing and more likely to bring in a $150 bid.

For Bombay Chai I called a girl who worked at David's firm as a paralegal—a gorgeous Indian woman named Madhu who was also a lesbian. Madhu had one of those faces that literally took your breath away—almond shaped dark eyes, dreamy smile—and then this mane of long black hair that coiled around her shoulder. She made grown men whine because she wasn't available and if you spent enough time with her you started thinking maybe being a lesbian wasn't such a bad thing. She and Gemma both agreed because they were cat lovers and we settled on the final weekend of July. It was fairly soon and it was a hot time to have people consider drinking hot tea, but Animal House wanted to get the central air system installed as soon as possible so that August would be less oppressive in the shelter.

As promised, Abigail came through with a caterer who would donate tea sandwiches and pastries, and a florist who would provide white and red streaked lilies for each table. All I had to do was have the tea on hand and write the profiles. But immediately, because as soon as they were finished the targeted mailing had to go out.

It took me awhile to focus and get into a writing rhythm, but after the first one was done I breezed through the rest. I made every tea sound sexy and enticing and how could you resist the sultry darkness of Chocolate Velvet, the gentle, undulating power of Russian Caravan or the unleashed force of Green Lychee? I was actually laughing as I finished up and showed the descriptions to Mike when he came in. We had planned to go mattress shopping since David had finally taken the bed and his other possessions away, and after we brought the mattress back Mike and I had intended to try it out together. Before we left, however, he skimmed over what I had written and for some reason just blew up over it all. Firstly, I think he was ticked because he wasn't being included and Joe was (Joe had agreed to be Russian Caravan and had even opted to put male *and* female preferences down for his tea companion), but as I explained to Mike, he was Assam tea and Assam was a shade too intense for most palates. I tried to compliment him by noting that the word Assam meant peerless or without rival and that I preferred to keep him to myself, but he wasn't buying. I'm not sure what set him off about the tea profiles, since they were just sexy, not pornographic, but he fumed and slammed the pages down.

"I don't like you thinking about these other guys like this," he snapped. "How would you like it if I were writing about coffee and Sumatra is one steamy sex-pot with bodacious curves and wouldn't you like her to fill your cup on a cold night?"

"I'd think that was pretty creative phrasing," I said. "Seriously. Do you have any suggestions to add to these?"

"No. I only suggest that you don't take part in any of it," he muttered. "I don't like the idea and I don't like that Abigail chick either."

I knew that Mike and Abigail wouldn't get along. I could see him dismissing her as a sharp-tongued bitch and her relegating him to a macho shithead level and almost as if through negative polarity, they had each acted like that around each other when they'd been introduced. Abigail was more caustic and aloof than ever and Mike was domineering and possessive. And he clearly wasn't letting down the defenses yet.

"I'm not taking part," I objected. "I'm not one of the teas, I'm just coordinating the tea services. Refilling hot water and bringing more napkins. Is that all right or do you want me to dress like a Muslim woman so that nobody can see my face and body?"

"Don't wise off to me," he cautioned.

"Then don't give me ultimatums."

He looked at me with an almost hurt or afraid expression—I only saw it for a second but then it disappeared and his eyes turned hard and distant.

"This isn't working," he said suddenly, shaking his head. "We're on different frequencies, you don't understand me and I don't get you. We should cut it off before we're in too deep. I'm sorry."

And then he walked. I sat there, dumbfounded, absently noting by the clock that the entire argument and break-up had only taken eleven minutes. I was going to let it slide and just try to get my bearings again, because this was so out of the blue, but then I turned furious. I called up Mike and left a message about how he was a stupid son-of-a-bitch and how dare he terminate something without hearing from me and if he was a non-negotiating my way or the highway jerk, he could go screw himself. And I hoped that that was all he'd find to screw for a long time. I didn't feel better after I'd left the message but I did feel like my head was less likely to explode and a steam valve had been opened to ease the pressure. Yet then I sat in the empty space where my new mattress was supposed to have been and cried. In the middle of the tears, the phone rang. It was Mike.

"Please don't do this tea thing, Liz," he said quietly. "Don't force my hand."

I regained my rage. "Don't ask me not to do it—are you completely crazy? What is the big *deal*?"

But once more we weren't negotiating because he hung up. I called him back and added a few more hateful things, hung up myself, longed for his body, then decided to go shop for my own mattress and have it delivered. I made sure to drop off the tea profiles to Abigail on the way. She scanned them quickly then said they were perfect and that the mailing could go out the day after tomorrow, right on schedule.

"Are you all right?" she asked, just when I was leaving. "You look upset."

I was out of it, I could tell. But I had been kicked in the stomach before with this type of abrupt shock so I knew how to handle myself. "I'm fine," I lied, keeping a forward momentum toward the door. Besides, perhaps Mike had been right—we were obviously on different wavelengths and cutting it off as soon as possible was the only sensible thing to do.

A few days later, Joe came over with a bunch of assorted biscotti and a caramel macchiato. And when I say biscotti I mean Joe's homemade biscotti, which weren't all hard and like plaster in your mouth but crumbly and supple, sopping up every drop of coffee and melding with its flavor. He said they were a peace offering and that he thought Mike had picked the fight with me because he was afraid of the relationship.

"You terrify him, Liz," he went on. "He thinks you think he's stupid or not sophisticated enough…he's got a major complex where you're concerned."

"Then he is stupid," I sighed. "I tell him all the time how handsome he is, how desirable, that he's street-smart and sharp and sensitive. I'm sorry, I can't be pussyfooting around him constantly, Joe."

"Give it some space," Joe advised. "He's going through a lot of changes and they're making him edgy. First he suddenly has a chance with you, after he'd pretty much given up, then he finds out about me, then he gets a chance to go into another business but he has to invest more cash than he wants to."

"What other business?" I asked.

"He might team up with a guy from the old neighborhood and they'd rehab buildings and houses, handle all the electrical and interior work as well as the decorating and stuff like tiled steam rooms or marble fireplaces," Joe said. "This would be to a buyer's specifications. Like finding a claw foot tub if somebody wants one, or lead glass windows or porcelain doorknobs…you know how it goes. They could turn a big profit because Home Depot-mania or not, not everybody wants to do all that on their own."

"That's a great idea," I said. "He rehabbed his own place so well. He has great skills, to be able to do the structural work and handle the style aspects too."

"I know, I know," Joe nodded. "But he has to put up a lot of cash to start, and he won't really be around to help with the Napoli. Still, he's too restless for this kind of life," he added. "I think you and I like it, we enjoy the pace and the regular customers and being part of the neighborhood, but Mike needs more action and variety."

"You're definitely right," I said. "He has too much energy. He needs to be tearing down things then rebuilding them. He needs to be on a crusade charging into salvage shops looking for 1920 kitchen faucet handles or pressed tin ceilings. Mike is a focused maniac."

"Amen to that," Joe laughed and then he squeezed my hand. "See, Liz, you know and understand my brother's insanity. You have to stay with him. It's like your civic duty."

I was about to object but the phone rang and I went to answer. It was Abigail, saying that we had our first tea check.

"And it's for four hundred and fifty hundred dollars!" she gushed. "Three times the asking price. She's a wealthy old lady and she loves Animal House. She also wants some of that Russian Caravan Man."

We had included photos of the tea mates in the mailing. Abigail had taken a good shot of Joe looking slightly raffish with one eyebrow raised.

"Oh my God, you were bought!" I yelled to Joe, who jerked back, startled. "This old lady paid an extra three hundred just for one sitting! You're the first to be booked." I licked my forefinger, reached out and pretended to touch him while making a hissing noise. "You are smoking hot, Joe. You're a tea gigolo dream."

Joe exhaled heavily with relief. "Good, she's old…maybe she'll be half-deaf and won't know how boring I am."

I hung up with Abigail and turned to him, exasperated.

"What is it with you and your brother?" I asked. "You're both so down on yourselves. Only in your case it's more appealing and modest. But please stop, you'll be fine."

He glanced at me hopefully. "I was really first? Before all those other much better looking, more interesting people?"

I shrugged. "You were first, I don't know why. You're such an ugly dogface loser. Maybe she's half-blind too. But she opened up her moneybags and said I'm jumping on the Russian Caravan, get out of my way."

Joe smiled, stepping aside to let a customer purchase a half-pound of Peach Darjeeling and an infuser.

"All right, I gotta get back to the ranch," he said. "Listen, Liz," he stressed again before leaving. "Don't give up on Mike. You know there's more to come for you both. Together. You can't escape so easily."

"He needs to apologize," I insisted. "This was his fight and his fault."

"He's too stubborn," Joe replied. "But he is like a piñata…once you crack it open, all sorts of sweet stuff comes out."

"Really. Can I use a baseball bat or a big stick to bust a hole in him?" I asked and Joe said that whatever worked was fine and that he also hoped that he, Joe, was not now mobbed on the street. Since he was so gorgeous and all. Since he had become the Russian Caravan Man.

CHAPTER 14

❀

It was a week before the big Teatime and two weeks into the fight with Mike and I still hadn't heard from him. I also noted that the Mustang convertible of his former Bermuda traveling companion Brandee (I had thought her name was spelled with a y but saw her vanity license plate with the EE) was parked outside the Napoli one evening and I figured he had gone back to his airhead comfort zone. If I had to act ditzy and submissive to keep Mike, I didn't want him. I forced all memories of the sex away and thanked God I hadn't broken up with David for his sake. I hadn't heard from David either except an occasional sorrowful call about forwarding his mail, so I congratulated myself on ending two romantic situations within a single month and shifted energies towards moving on.

One morning I felt unusually happy, like I had drunk from some magic sparkling spring. I was dazzled by how blue the sky was and how perfectly formed the clouds were, and I looked around the tearoom and loved it all too—the ruddy gloss of the wood floors, my mother's paintings, the samovars, the combined perfumes of Passionfruit Ceylon (Table 2) and Ginger Spice (Table 4). I felt like it was one of those special, charged moments when something incredibly special was about to happen, and I thought I will meet quite a man today, I just know it. And about half an hour later a man did come in and walk toward me, and he was handsome and magnetic with bedroom eyes—and he was also my damn half-brother from Ypsilanti, Michigan. There are times that you hear that phrase *I almost jumped out of my skin*, but at that instant I truly perceived what it was about.

"Hello," he said, glancing around. "Nice place. How are you doing? Remember me, my name is Benny Fonseca?"

He was wearing a ripped tie-dye tank top and long khaki shorts with leather desert sandals. I saw Thea's head whip around at the sight of him because he was very much up her alley.

"Leave me alone, I'm your sister, get out of here now!" I almost yelled, with a further insane urge to make the sign of the cross like he was a vampire. But he already knew. He explained quietly, to avoid Thea's pricked up ears, that he had seen me slip with Mike and his father into his father's private office and that later he had asked him what that had been about. He and his father were close and his father had almost seemed to want to tell someone about me, so they had discussed it and decided to keep it to themselves.

"What's a family without a few juicy secrets anyway?" Benny concluded, no longer speaking softly. "Boring as hell."

"Bo-ring," I repeated, remembering how he had said that Ann Arbor got like that every now and then so he would come down to Chicago. "So you're visiting friends?"

"I am," he confirmed. "I know some guys in a band here—they're called Dangerous Toys. Ever heard of them?"

"I have," Thea interrupted. She was clearing off a table and if she leaned over any more her firm white mammies were definitely going to tumble out of what could be liberally described as a shirt.

"She's a friendly wench," Benny observed. "How does she know I'm not here to see you? As a suitor." He smiled and I noticed how he really looked like his father, our father, whoever's father, around the mouth then and how there was also a similarity between us around the eyes and I relaxed. It was like a line went up, shifting him from scary taboo incest potential to my Other Brother. I had another brother now and he was the total suave, openly expressive opposite of Pete and that was fascinating. Not that I would ever love Pete less but it was just like finding another color in the spectrum.

"Thea still thinks I'm with Mike probably," I said. "I don't confide in her much. Plus I doubt she sees you as my type of suitor. You're her type of suitor and that's all she wants to know. Would you like some tea? Anything to eat?"

Benny nodded. "Sure. Mango on ice, please. And maybe some zucchini bread."

Mango, that made sense. I would have typed him as Blackberry or Mango Ceylon definitely. He watched while I fixed just that, then he came around to the back of the counter and sat on a stool so that we could talk more. "Why aren't you with Mike?" he asked. "Dad really liked him."

Dad, I thought, almost jumping up and down like a five year old. He used the word *Dad* and it pertains to *me*.

"He said Mike was the kind of guy who would take a bullet for his love," Benny continued, and I knew that was true but I refused to start getting soft on Mike again. Because Mike now had Brand-ee and could take a bullet for her. Otherwise it might rupture one of her implants.

"He's a hothead," I complained. "And he always wants to tell you what to do." I gave him a brief synopsis of our fight.

"Well, that's the other side of taking a bullet for you," Benny said. "Intensity. And if he is with a dumb blonde now it's just to salvage his ego. He won't forget you that easily, I'm sure."

"He can forget me," I said. "And vice versa. The sooner the better."

"Now that's anger talking," Benny guessed. "You both looked pretty happy together. Even if you stay apart, I doubt you'll want to forget him in the long run. Every encounter has its unique meaning."

Good Lord, this guy is beyond the opposite of Pete, I thought: he's the Official Anti-Pete. Thea was about to climax on the sidelines and I just smiled. It was good to be connected to someone like him. We decided to make dinner together on Sunday so that we could whip up a few Portuguese dishes and talk about *Dad*, who Benny said was planning to send me something.

"I think it's a photo of my grandmother…you know, the one you look like," he guessed. "When she was younger. He must be getting it reprinted because he said it wasn't ready this time around. And I had to get down here right away, I met this amazing girl who works at Circus nightclub…she rides the trapeze."

Thea slammed down a chair in disgust and muttered that she was taking her break. Benny grinned.

"I just said I'd met her…I didn't say she was the only girl in the city," he sighed, but I told him he might want to tell that to Thea on his way out and see how she felt about sharing.

By the end of Sunday night I had several old family recipes for a family I wasn't quite part of, and some delicious leftovers of the *galinha estufada* Benny had made (chicken stew made with white wine, potatoes, new peas, paprika and curry) and kale soup, which tastes a lot better than it sounds. I had also learned a few phrases of the family lingo, which Benny and his brother and sister had had to learn—there was no option. I could say *somos todos Portuguese* (we are all Portuguese); *bom dia* and *boa tarde* (good morning and good afternoon); and *tchau*, which was used like Ciao. While we were cooking we had listened to the Gilberto and Gilberto record and Benny had laughed because he had always made fun of that album and called it When Dad Had Hair and Groovy Boots. He had brought it to Show and Tell in the fifth grade and said that his teacher, who had previously hated him for being a brat, got all dreamy over the music and gave him an A+.

Benny told me that Gilberto had met his mother right after goofing around with my mother, and that his mother had gotten pregnant too with Benny, only their affair had ended in marriage. But his father really loved his mother and always said she was like a wonderful, smart, bossy, fiery drill sergeant who kept everybody in line. His mother was from a poorer family and had been ambitious and driven, which was why she was one of the top Portuguese language professors in the country, but Gilberto had come from some wealth and had a very broad education in all areas, including music, so he was more laid-back.

"He likes to stop and smell the roses," Benny commented. "Every single one of them…then he tends to get lost in the garden every once in awhile. That's why he's so great when he plays at the restaurant, because he just riffs off the basic songs he knows and can go on for hours. I swear he never seems to play the same stuff twice. In all these years I've been listening to Dad from the bar, I never get sick of the music."

He scraped the last of the kale soup into a Tupperware container and looked at me gravely. "My brother Marco plays a set pattern of songs—he's so rigid and boring even though he thinks he's hot shit. I hate to tell you this but I'm not fond of my brother. He's too into money and commercialization. He wants to turn our restaurant into a franchise then sell out." Benny sighed. "We'll be having some ugly fights in the future, when Dad retires."

"What about your sister?" I asked. "Do you get along with her?"

"She's okay," Benny said. "Her name is Elena and she works for a Brazilian import company in Manhattan. Although she was a big snitch when she was younger and she still can be that way. Like if Dad ever told her about you and the thing with your mother she'd run right to our Mom and spill it. I'm really glad I met you," he added, smiling. "It's like you're one of us, like you belong more on the subversive side with me and Dad."

"Even though I have to hide on the subversive sidelines," I reminded.

Benny lifted his shoulders philosophically then yawned. "Maybe, but he and I still know you're there, so what else matters? Can I crash on your couch?" he asked. "I'm exhausted and I want to take off early tomorrow morning, back to Ann Arbor. If I go back to the Dangerous Toys house I'll end up partying. They tend to all come to life at around six p.m. then play somewhere and stay up until dawn. Which is a great lifestyle if you're not part of a family business."

"Sure you can stay." I threw him some clean sheets and towels. "But what's happening with the trapeze artist?"

"She's working tonight," he said. "The show must go on."

"Did you call Thea?" I asked, just out of curiosity.

He laughed. "Thea told me right off that she does not take sloppy seconds. If you want to date her, you date exclusively her."

"Oh, that doesn't surprise me," I said. "I think Thea's more of an old-fashioned girl than she admits."

"With a tongue stud," Benny noted.

"Well, it's an exclusive tongue stud," I laughed. "She doesn't use it on just anyone."

The phone rang but I let it go to the machine; it was Abigail, like I expected. Abigail generally called at least once a day to give me an update on how things were progressing or to suggest something new, and now she was advising that Chocolate Velvet had dropped out and we needed a replacement immediately.

"Who's Chocolate Velvet?" Benny asked. "A horse? Is that woman your bookie, Liz? Are you a secret racetrack junkie?"

I was disappointed. The Chocolate Velvet Man had been a fine-looking Jamaican medical student with a lilting accent and to be honest, if I'd had to choose my own special tea companion, he would have been the one. I explained the event to Benny, who nodded while chewing on a hangnail. Which wasn't the most appealing or seductive thing, but still Benny had those dark lambent eyes and the smooth, low-key charm. He could definitely be Chocolate Velvet tea.

"Can you come back here next weekend?" I asked.

He looked apprehensive. "I don't know for sure…weekends are busy at Fado. Dad will let me off if he knows the reason but stupid Marco'll be wondering why."

"Never mind," I said. "I don't want to cause any family strife."

"Yeah, but it shouldn't be such an issue. What the hell," he complained irritably. "Here I'm twenty-eight years old and I have to explain every move I make to my brother. And my mother still, to a certain extent. She's can get on my case."

"She's not like my mother," I laughed. "When I was fifteen I got sick of her flaking around so I told her I was running away. She said that was fine but I should wait a few days until the moon was in Sagittarius, so it would be a better time to start a new journey. And don't think she was trying to psych me out…she was serious. I only stayed just to spite her. And because she kept letting my brother wear pajamas to school and that just wasn't a good idea. He was really comfortable in pajamas and kept falling asleep in class."

"That's nice…meanwhile I had a nine o'clock curfew," Benny challenged. "Do you know what that's like in high school? Major social stigma. I remember in the summer the damn sun hadn't even set but I had to hurry home. Then *my* mother would check my breath for alcohol and shine a flashlight into my eye pupils to test for drugs. I'm surprised she didn't have me peeing in a cup too."

"Interesting," I said. "You seemed to belong more with my family and I would have been better off with yours."

"I don't know…I guess the grass is always greener when you don't have to mow someone else's lawn." Benny yawned again. "But count me in for next week. I want to do this and I will."

"It's just a charity tea," I reminded. "Not worth causing a feud."

"It shouldn't rate a feud," he persisted. "I can get a perfectly good sub to bartend for me and besides, I'm the eldest male of the house. That little fart Marco should have more respect." He stretched out on the couch and began to untie his Biblical nomad sandals. "Hey, can you get me a glass of ice water, Liz? With a twist of lime?" he asked. "Possa-o receber me um vidro de água?" he repeated in Portuguese, imitating those male robot voices that tend to be on language instruction tapes. "Minha cara irmã? That means my sister. My *dear* sister. Or maybe I could call you Elzira. That's the closest match for your name."

I smiled. "Do you want me to treat you like a guest or like my other brother Pete?"

He raised an eyebrow. "What would you say to Pete?"

"Get your own ice water and/or are your legs broken?"

"I'd like to be treated as a guest," Benny replied promptly, and then he reached for the t.v. remote and turned on *Wild Chicago*, sound blaring, and just like Pete I went right in, took the remote, asked if he was deaf, helpless *and* broken-legged and turned the volume down.

CHAPTER 15

❀

I went with Abigail to take a look at Animal House and to meet the main person in charge, a high-strung ball of energy named Lucinda who ran around putting drops in sick cats' ears and giving flea dips to collies while we talked. I was exhausted just following her, but was glad I had seen the actual premises because it made me want to give a charity tea every week. There's something so trusting and open about an animal. I'm not a particularly religious person and I still throw all the Baptist literature my sister sends me right into the trash, but when you see how much pets can care for us and how they want to be with people, you have to wonder whether they really might be gifts from God.

Abigail had to leave because she was borderline asthmatic, but I hung around the cat section of the shelter and held a few of the bigger boys so that Lucinda could trim their claws. She warned me about a muscular black cat with amber eyes and a sleek presence—that he might be a little surly—but when I held him he just looked up and relaxed and let her do her thing. He was a neutered male who'd been found hanging around a gas station; she said she guessed he was about four years old. His name was Licorice.

"Wow, he likes you," she noted. "Generally we have some behavior problems with Licorice. He's a tough guy."

Licorice was still on my lap, purring, though he did reach out to whap a passing cat in the face for no particular reason. Lucinda went to break up a scuffle between two calicos while I stroked Licorice's ears. He licked at my fingers and chewed gently on my bracelet. And then he stared imploringly and I knew I wouldn't be able to leave without him.

"You're a feline Mike, aren't you?" I said. The cat stood up and nuzzled my throat, and then he smacked at yet another cat who tried to move in on his turf.

"Okay, now it's clear that you're Mike and I should absolutely not take you home," I laughed, but I still had Lucinda draw up the paperwork and get him ready to go. And while anytime you had called him Licorice he would turn back disgustedly like, please, I cannot possibly answer to something so stupid, once I started calling him Mike he looked at me with total comprehension. When he first got to my apartment he prowled around uncertainly, low to the ground, then ate a few bits of white meat from Benny's chicken stew and sniffed at the furniture and decided it wasn't a bad place. He was very territorial and wouldn't let me out of his sight, and if someone came up the landing stairs he ran to the door to protect me, like a watchdog, while at night he slept next to me on the empty pillow so that nothing could get me while I slept.

After a couple days of this I began to seriously long for Mike the Man, not the cat, because I missed his quirky sexy ways. It still seemed ridiculous to have ended it over tea, but I refused to call him. I wanted him again in body and mind, but I wouldn't be able to do it if I caved or pretended that the fight didn't matter, because it really did. It was an issue of independence and respect. And of him not being such a damn tyrant.

So even though all that longing and lusting was twisting through my body, I decided that if it was meant to be it would and I wasn't going to force it. I had felt that way when I'd left my father's restaurant and he had gotten in touch through Benny not even three weeks later. Sometimes even though it's the most difficult course of action, you just have to let something go—otherwise it has no chance to come back to you. That extends beyond even a spiritual philosophy; it's scientific too. I read once that people overwhelmed with problems had been asked to sit in front of a suspended magnet and try to figure out a solution to their issues. When they did, the magnet remained where it was, but when they were told to just completely give up and let whatever happen, the energy field would shift and the magnet would move toward them.

I pet Mike, Jr. like I was in a trance, over and over.

"I am letting *go*," I said, imagining the psychic transfer of all anxiety and need onto him. Into that thick black fur. He jumped off and began to preen himself irritably after about five minutes; I guess even he didn't want to have to deal with that business.

I then cleaned the apartment and made a final list of things to do, since the tea was tomorrow. There was a cricket somewhere in the living room and it was driving Mike, Jr. insane as he tried to push himself behind the couch to get at it. Then he seemed to think it was in the couch itself and was halfway crammed within the valley of the cushions when the doorbell rang. The cat froze, then went charging into the foyer to stand watch.

Apparently the magnet had moved back toward me. It was Mike, carrying a box of stuff from the Napoli and a few red and peach carnations. He looked nervous and stiff, though the stiffness turned out to be more from a pulled hamstring muscle, he said, which had happened the other day when he'd fallen off a scaffold.

"I don't know what to tell you," he sighed, shaking his head. "I was an extreme super-size idiot, I wasn't thinking. You don't have to let me in…I just thought I'd stop by and see if you'd have tea with me, at eight o'clock at night. What's that tea you said I remind you of?"

"Assam," I answered, trying not to laugh, because even though we would probably get into another fight about what we had been fighting about, I had never been so glad to see anyone in my life.

"Is that because it begins with Ass?"

"Could be," I reasoned. "I never thought of that."

"Do you have any?"

"I think so."

Mike, Jr. had begun to sniff at Mike's shoes. "Who this?" he said. "When did you get a cat?"

"On Tuesday. From the animal shelter we're helping out with the tea." I let Mike in while the cat followed him with stealthy suspicion.

"He's pretty fierce," Mike observed. "He must have trained with the Guardian Angels. I can respect a cat like this."

"The cat's a lot like you," I said. "That's why his name is Mike, Jr. He's a little psychotic. What did you bring?" I asked, nodding to the box. I was pretending to be casual and at ease, like this didn't matter to me at all and I had no intense desire to throw myself at him and the build I had missed so much—even down to the Playboy tattoo. He was limping, though, and I don't know that he could have handled being tackled. He said that he had brought some of Joe's biscotti, ham and roasted pepper sandwiches, and ricotta puffs.

"Is that okay for tea?"

"Sounds pretty good to me," I said, and we bumped around each other awkwardly in the kitchen while he transferred the food onto plates and I put the carnations in a vase. I also made the tea, let it steep and poured it into a pair of garnet glass cups.

"These are from Ebay," I noted. "One dollar each."

"Where's your opal?" Mike asked, easing painfully into a chair. "Did you chuck it down the sewer?"

"No, I'm just not wearing it now," I said. "But I would never throw it away."

He stared at my throat and I stared at his eyes and mouth. The food seemed inconsequential for a minute but then I thought no, don't jump right into bed with him, let him wait. Wait at least an *hour*, for God's sake. Think of Brandee and how he didn't waste any time getting back to knocking boots with her.

He pointed to the cat, standing vigilantly by the table.

"This is like a prison visit," Mike laughed. "You're not slipping me any cocaine or contraband, not while he's around." He tossed a scrap of ham to Mike, Jr., who pounced on it before it even hit the rug. "Hey, look the other way, Turnkey."

"Now he'll be your friend for life," I said.

"How about you?" he asked, brushing his fingertips against my own. "Can you be my friend again?"

"What about Brandee?" I queried back. "I saw her car outside the Napoli. Is she your friend too?"

He stared into his tea. "I called her, yeah, but I couldn't go through with it. It's like she's waiting for something serious even though she acts like a bimbo, and it's not fair...I'm not interested in much more than sex where she's concerned. It's not like how I feel about you."

"You don't have to lie, Mike," I advised. "If you were with her, it's not my business."

"I wasn't with her; end of story," he said tersely, then he sipped the tea. At first he winced like you tend to wince when you initially taste Assam, but then he drank more. "So this is how I am to you, as a tea," he noted. "Because I don't think it's bad, but do you like it?"

"I do, I just need to put in some milk and brown sugar," I said. "Assam is hard to take straight. But it really gets you going when you do drink it. I tend to like stronger varieties...I'm not so into herbal infusions or even jasmine or green tea."

"That's good for me, I guess," he said, handing me a ricotta puff, which was like a traditional cheese puff but creamier. And they were still warm, so that the outer golden shell dissolved in your mouth. The cat looked expectantly at Mike.

"That's enough for now, mooch, wait until we're done," he said, but he threw him another piece of ham anyway. I refilled our cups.

"I've missed having you in my life, Liz," Mike said. I nodded.

"I've missed you too," I whispered, feeling strangely shy and vulnerable. And a bit heady, to be honest, to be drinking Assam in the presence of someone so like Assam. (You'd definitely have to be a tea freak to understand.) So dark and virile, the full impact of the bouquet tightening the inside of your cheeks, just like if you were to kiss Mike your mouth would contract as he flicked his tongue in and out. He had always gotten to me with that tongue—everywhere.

A few seconds later I had my hands in his hair and was licking olive oil and Dijon mustard off his lips and I knew the craziness had started again but I didn't care. He moved cautiously and slowly because of the hamstring and for awhile it reminded me of an old time roller coaster I had ridden once, with the rickety car creaking up the wooden tracks then pausing at the top. We had just sat there waiting for gravity to tip us forward, and it seemed like it might not happen, like you'd be stuck at the top forever, but then suddenly you were flying downward and screaming and rattling to the bottom again. Which was fine for me, but it seemed like he was seriously hurting.

"Mike, don't force yourself," I urged right before he was through, but he said something about wanting to play through the pain and that was the end of that.

Afterward I made a hot compress of towels and wrapped it around the back of his leg, then I gave him some juice so he could take one of the Tylenol and codeine pills the E.R. doctor had prescribed.

"Don't worry about me…I should go," he said, trying to get up but not succeeding. "You need to sleep, you've got that tea tomorrow. You shouldn't be Nancy Nurse."

He closed his eyes and I admired his chest, shoulders, the line of his jaw. He had a strong jaw that jutted out and indicated stubbornness; I remembered Joe telling me that Mike was stubborn and hard to crack, but once you did so all kinds of sweet stuff would come out. I still didn't think you could crack him at once, however, but instead it seemed like it would be more of a gradual process over time. Like chiseling marble or granite.

"What made you come over tonight, Mike?" I asked, wondering if that would set him off or he would tell me the truth. He opened his eyes and looked at me.

"When I fell off the scaffolding the other day, there was a weird interval before I landed and I was thinking Christ, I'm going to break my back and be paralyzed," he said. "It wasn't like my life flashed before my eyes, but that thought did like some blinding white lightning bolt. Then when I sat up and saw I was okay, that I had only done minor damage, what was happening with you seemed very stupid. It seemed stupid to keep staying away, but I knew that the longer I did, the less likely you'd be let me in. So that's why I didn't even call, I just came over. I didn't want to start thinking about it too much again, that we're not alike, that there might be problems. I just wanted to think about what was there—do you know what I mean? Is it still there for you?"

I smiled because the painkiller was kicking in and he was becoming groggy, struggling to stay awake and wait for my answer.

"It's there and we're not that different," I insisted. "Especially when you're like this."

"Doped up?" he asked.

"Doped up, thoughtful, more relaxed…it's all fine by me."

"Goodnight, baby," he said, groping around for my hand. I held his for a moment then took the compresses off his leg before they had a chance to get clammy. From the other room the cricket began to chirp and trill, stopping as the cat circled the couch and pounced at shadows around it, then starting up again, like a mini-nature soundtrack for the night.

When I woke Mike was gone, which was surprising because I was a light sleeper and not much got past me. I wondered whether I had been so keyed up lately that to sleep with him had been incredibly relaxing, through both his physical presence and in having had sex. That or I was finally getting used to my new too-firm mattress. Whatever the case, before leaving he had tacked a note to the refrigerator which read:

Good luck today.
Hope I'll see you later, Lizzie.
Love, Mike.

It was a simple note but from Mike it spoke volumes. Cooperation, consideration, conciliation. Perhaps he had left the toilet seat up but he had also done the tea dishes, and dishes were ten times more important than toilets. I fed Mike the Cat and grabbed a piece of string away before he ate that too, then I took a shower. I decided to wear a red paisley top with a scoop neck and fished the opal out of my jewelry box to complement it. It really was a pretty stone, and the finest chain I had ever seen. I thought of that song again, from the CD I played at Samovar so often:

> *Fibrous and snaring*
> *And in his daring*
> *I found his bed.*

> *He was much more*
> *Than I demanded*
> *Have to be candid*
> *It works for me.*

To think of the lyrics now, though, didn't depress me. They just seemed to fit, like the opal itself no longer made me feel sad or guilty. I was going to twist my hair into its usual nape-knot but decided to leave it down instead, to let it flow. Sometimes it looked better down, I figured. Sometimes it was better just to be a slightly different somebody, especially when that other person seemed to be becoming me.

CHAPTER 16

The tea began with a minor crisis, even though Abigail started frothing at the mouth and acting like it was the end of the world. Gemma had called and left an awful message that you could barely hear because she was so weak, and in essence the gist of it was that she had a migraine and couldn't make the event.

"Is she just pretending?" Abigail accused. "Migraines can be psychosomatic…and she seemed hesitant about doing it the other day. Is she being bashful and screwing us over? How *dare* she pull this last minute bullshit!" she yelled. "Doesn't she know that everything was in place and now it's out of *order*? What about your other waitress?"

"Thea's not scheduled to work today and I doubt she would, just out of spite," I guessed. "She was peeved because I asked Gemma to do this event and not her. She's not the forgiving kind either."

"Tell her that you will fire her," Abigail instructed. "If she doesn't show up. Don't *ask* her, command."

"Abigail, I don't pay either one of those girls enough to command anything. I'm surprised they've even stayed with me this long, considering the turnover rate in jobs like theirs," I said. "That's not a fair request."

"Not fair," Abigail repeated, like it was a foreign phrase she didn't quite comprehend. She stood there like some Fruit Stripe gum harridan in her mod rainbow mini-dress, which was a perfect style for her and looked cute, but the facial expression was complete raving loon.

"All right, then what do you have to say about this, Liz!" she went on. "The event is starting in seventy-three minutes and we have no Rose Congou!"

"Well, first of all," I said as I went around the room laying out jacquard napkins, plates, cups and saucers. "Calm the hell down, Abigail. No one's going to the gas chamber over this, we'll just find a substitute. If worse comes to worse you or I can sit in for that service. Or we can refund the damn money. Gemma is a great employee and she's never missed a day of work, so she must be very sick. I'm not even going to question her on it."

"Yes, but if you sit in for the service, who'll be serving the *tea*?" she exploded. "And I suppose I can sit in but I wasn't the one in the brochure picture, I'm not what they chose specifically. I hate inconsistencies."

You're also nothing like that lovely, enchanting tea, I thought, especially in your present rabid condition. I must have given her a heavy look then because she came down a few levels and apologized.

"I'm sorry," she murmured. "It's just that I pride myself on being perfect and putting on perfect events. I can deal with change all throughout the planning of something but when it's so close to start time, I tend to snap."

"Well, I hope that Benny doesn't oversleep or have car trouble, since he's coming in from Michigan," I said, which set her off again.

"Is that possible?" she demanded. "I mean, was I supposed to get two or three *understudies* for all of these people because they can't show up at an assigned spot for two freaking hours of their life?"

"I don't know…maybe!" I laughed back. "Shit happens—haven't you ever seen the bumper sticker?"

She clearly decided that I was too vulgar to deal with, did not respond and instead began riffling through her huge day-timer to find a replacement. Until I stopped her because I had a thought way out of leftfield, and since I rarely get those I try not to ignore them.

"Let me call someone," I said, dialing my brother's number. The leftfield idea was for Vivienne, Joe's former green card bride, to be Rose Congou, even though the last time I had seen her she'd been a bossy tipsy nymphomaniac. But she was strawberry blonde and very pretty, with a warm blush to her skin. I had also been talking to my brother about Vivienne over the past month and she actually sounded like she was rather charming. Intelligent, appealing—and she had a French accent, what more did anyone need.

By some small miracle, not only was Pete home, Vivienne was with him and she said she'd love to help the pussycats and would be there in half an hour. She showed up in a pink dress with black satin gloves, black stockings, a temporary rose shoulder tattoo and pink lipstick as her "interpretation" of Rose Congou (she was after all, a Parisian fashion design student) and for as much as I loved Gemma, Vivienne's appearance and entire demeanor was fantastic. She was like a tranquilizer dart going into Abigail's neck and we regrouped and all began again, on a mellower note.

Joe was in place, looking rather suave himself with a newly grown soul-patch and a touch of pomade glistening in his hair, which wasn't even mussed when Vivienne pounced on him to give him a kiss. Then Benny showed up in soft brown suede, also looking fabulous, then Madhu, the paralegal from David's firm took her seat as Chai in a cerise silk sheath. Madhu was a total stunner as usual; Vivienne, Joe and Benny were perfect; Winston Tsiao, the Green Lychee martial arts guy was something else in his olive hand-tailored suit from Hong Kong…and the only dud I would have noted was Abigail's choice for Earl Grey. His name was Geoff and he wasn't even British, he was just affected, with a haughty way of surveying things and a constant need to make sly unfunny commentary. I felt sorry for whoever had paid a hundred and fifty bucks for him because while what I served would be genuine, Geoff himself had that tang of cheaper Earl Grey that doesn't seem to be flavored with bergamot but tastes more tea sprayed with Lemon Pledge.

And so we began. The weather was unusually cooperative for the last day of July, since it was no longer muggy and in the mid-nineties but had cooled to a reasonable seventy-eight degrees, which made the concept of hot tea less nauseating yet still allowed for an iced brew. Abigail and Lucinda from Animal House took a table on the sidelines while I went around unobtrusively, explaining our tea service offerings and detailing each tea itself and how it complemented the man or woman at the table. Joe was still nervous so I just gently touched his shoulder; Benny was trying to make me laugh while I talked so I had to tune him out; Vivienne whispered discreetly to me that she thought my brother was watching her from the car with the binoculars my mother had given him, which he was; I ignored Geoff's insistence upon being called *Lord Earl Spank-a-Lot* for the rest of the afternoon; and I saw how Winston Tsiao was discreetly giving Joe the eye.

Abigail's caterer had brought orange peel scones, chicken curry, olive cucumber and basil chevre finger sandwiches, then mini chocolate rum balls and peach caramel tarts for dessert. I placed each three-tiered tea tray on the tables, poured tea through silver strainers and kept an ear on the music, shifting CDs of harp songs, Nick Drake, Billie Holiday, Chopin, Gilberto and Gilberto (Pete had burned a disk of the album for me, which was convenient because I didn't always have my Close and Play turntable along), which again had Benny trying to make me crack a smile.

"What's with you?" he complained between sittings. "You're like one of those guys standing in front of Buckingham Palace. Bo-ring."

"I am being professional," I said. "Tea is my life."

"Want a clove cigarette real quick during your break?" he offered.

"No, I'll get all sleepy," I replied but I still took one for later.

Benny had no interest in me during his second round, which placed him with a seemingly prim blonde, but she had a good décolletage thing going and a husky laugh that he just couldn't get enough of. Joe was with another older woman, a former showgirl who said he reminded her of her third husband (third out of five, evidently, and she seemed to be looking at Joe as a possible Number 6); while Madhu had an equally attractive partner with whom she too was clearly connecting. I could see Geoff watching their every move and surely playing out girl on girl fantasies in his Lord Earl Sleaze-a-Lot head.

Vivienne had gone and screamed at my brother for spying during halftime and was now chatting with a portly man who dealt in antiques and who wanted her so bad I thought at any moment he was going to start offering up piles of gold doubloons or Ming vases. I went through my rounds once more and refreshed cups, whisked crumbs, and then just smiled and enjoyed watching this little pageantry unfold in a setting that had been pretty much of a tasseographic dream just a few short years ago. Tasseography is the art of reading tealeaves. I had seen the shape of a perfect oval form in my cup when I had first been thinking of Samovar, and an egg shape meant definite career success.

Towards the end of the tea, Abigail sidled up and gave me her old winning smile, her nose as flawless and straight as always but since I'd seen the full moon side to her I was a shade more wary.

"We should really plan more events like this," she whispered. "You're an ideal balance for me, because you're so level-headed and all. Would you like to plan more events together?"

"Uh, I'll have to think about it," I said, while in reality I was like no way, Jane, I'd rather stick my finger in a socket. I complimented her perfume as a distraction, because I did like it—it had a woodsy, fruity scent, almost like a fine tea.

"Oh, it's Mitsouko…here, have some." She spritzed my arm and throat with such a cloud that I almost sneezed. "Say, who's that man by the door? I meant to thank him, he's been telling people that this is a private event and Samovar's not open ever since we started."

I couldn't see whom she was talking about at first but figured it was either Pete or Mike, but when I craned my neck to look I caught a glimpse of David.

Which wasn't a huge surprise, that he would show up, because surely he'd known the tea was taking place either through Joe or Madhu or maybe he'd even read about it in the *Reader* or *New City*, but that he would stand by the door and try to be an active participant struck me as nervy. Since things were winding down on the tea service end, I excused myself and went to talk to him.

"What are you doing?" I asked, and while my voice was abrupt I wondered how long it would be before I could see David and not want to lean on his shoulder and feel like nothing could ever harm me in the world. Or, on the other hand, when I would stop feeling like he and that same happy world had betrayed me so much.

"I wanted to stop by," he said, smiling apologetically. "I was going to wait until after the guests had left but then some other people tried to walk in and I figured you didn't want to be interrupted. So I turned into the doorman. By the way, did you know your brother was watching with binoculars from his car? And not too secretly either."

I smiled too now, shaking my head. "I was advised of the situation. But you know, it's almost a good sign. That he's so crazy about a girl that he wants to play I Spy while she has tea with fat rich men. Before he just would have rolled a joint and pretended he didn't care."

"Yes, our little stoner is growing up, I guess. How've you been, Liz?" David then asked, peering into my face while I tried not to do the same to him. Though he did look better than when we'd last met, I was glad to note. Not so tense or drained, and he'd gotten some sun, which meant he'd hopefully spent a few days at the cabin and escaped that paper-lined cell he called an office.

"I'm all right," I answered. "And you?"

He shrugged. "Alive. Figuring it out as I go along. Madhu looks nice," he added, motioning to the scene inside. "And Joe." He glanced at me anxiously then, like I might be offended by the Joe comment. "I don't see or speak to him that often," he amended. "I just—"

"David, I don't care if you see Joe everyday," I said flatly. "I've never had a problem with Joe. I just don't want you to hurt him."

"Like I hurt you?" he asked.

"No," I corrected swiftly. "You can't hurt him in the same way because he wouldn't be shocked and surprised like I was, he knows what to expect. But you could still break his heart."

"Liz, I'm sorry—" he began, and he reached for my hand like he had thousands of times in the past but I couldn't take it, it seemed so familiar and it confused me so much that now I just wanted to smack him. Really hard, to knock his glasses clear off his head and also knock that pained martyr's smile off his face too.

"Stop it," I muttered, flinging him off. "Just stop…I can't keep going through this. We shouldn't see each other anymore—ever—or at least not for several *years* until there's some kind of healthy distance. And especially not now…this isn't the time or the place."

He took a step back, head bent, like he was reluctantly agreeing yet then he edged forward again and started to speak.

"I just want to say one more thing," he insisted but when I tried to leave he blocked my path. "And I'd appreciate it you'd hear me out because it has nothing to do with us. One of the main reasons I came here was to see Madhu, believe it or not."

"Why?" I sighed. "Do you like her now too?"

"I do," he challenged. "I've always found her attractive. She's dark like you and that's my type…no, don't interject now, please. At any rate, the other day I had a talk with her about the tea and how she could put down a preference whether she wanted to be with men or women, and how great it felt to choose women and not be ashamed. She comes from a very traditional Indian family in New Jersey, and they had picked out a husband for her and were making wedding arrangements but she couldn't go through with it. She tried to explain why but they were horrified with what she was telling them, and they pretty much kicked her out and declared her dead. Everyone she cared about in that family—grandmother, uncles, aunts, mother, father, sisters—just cut it clean. I think maybe she talks to one of her sisters but it's extremely strained and awkward, but the point is that she was hurt, she felt disgusted with herself at first, but then she got her bearings and took a job in Chicago and never looked back. And now here she is, as she is."

We both glanced inside to Madhu's table, where she sat holding her teacup in one hand while making eloquent gestures with the other. David continued: "There are assholes at work who treat her differently because she's openly lesbian and there are guys who are always trying to *turn* her back, but she keeps on and she never lets them wear her down." He laughed bitterly. "I don't know where she gets the courage. But I'm hoping to find half of it someday myself. I guess I only need half, right?"

I looked at David then almost with a healthy detachment. It was like the light had changed around him in a sense, because I suddenly saw how each of us had wanted to use the other as a shield—how he had seemed so perfect and sheltering for me and I had seemed so acceptably heterosexual for him. Like he would take all the conflict and intense emotion out of my world and I would take all the doubt and social stigma from his.

"David," I ventured. "I'm sure there are women in your situation who could agree to that arrangement you talked about. Marriage, children, everything. If you still want to go that route. I just can't do it myself."

"I know you can't," he said irritably. "I'm not asking you to. I'm not even sure why I'm here, but I hated how you left my office the last time I saw you, like you were running from a monster."

I looked at his wide eyes ringed with green and said that I hadn't been running from a monster, I'd been running from a prince. The one who I'd thought would love me comfortably and with reasonable passion, as well as handle all my legal matters and suggest which mutual fund to pick.

"I did do that, didn't I?" he said. "While we were together?"

I nodded. "That's why I was running."

The tea was breaking up beyond us and I could see Abigail making her announcements, thanking the caterer and the donors and the florist and frowning when she couldn't find me.

"I guess I should get back in there," I said. "Do you want to come too? Say hello to Joe or Madhu? Help me with the dishes?"

David considered it but then only offered to help with the dishes, and I brushed him off on that.

"No, you always make me dry them and I like to wash," I said. "Hot suds, watching the dirty become clean. Hydrotherapy, you can't beat it."

"Well, all right then, Alizarin," he smiled, straightening the strap of my long white apron. "You take care now. Don't be a stranger."

"Okay, David Kerplunky," I answered, because that was a story that David's mother was always telling me, how adorable her son had been playing his favorite game of Kerplunk as a little boy. Only she was always calling it Kerplunky. I was on the verge of crying but this time it wasn't with such anguish, it was more like leaving a place you had loved visiting so much but you couldn't live there.

"What's the hardest tea to swallow?" he asked, right before he left. I knew it was a riddle but couldn't come up with an answer.

"Reality," he said, walking on.

"Reality," I repeated in a hollow way, and then I went back inside.

CHAPTER 17

❀

When the tea was officially over and the lingerers drifting out the door and a total of $2,100 had been raised, surely a decent start on that central heating and cooling system for Animal House, I said goodbye to everyone and thanked them for coming. Joe noted that he had seen David and gave me a quizzical look, but I suggested to Joe that he just let David go for a while and if it was meant to be, the magnet would pull back to him. In the meantime he had gotten Winston Tsiao, Martial Arts Instructor's business card with an embossed dragon motif, so he was doing fine on his own. Abigail had flown out the door after the antiques dealer because she wanted to schmooze him into having a charity auction, and Pete had flown in the door to reclaim Vivienne, who pouted and pretended that she didn't like jealous men. Then ten seconds later she covered him with delirious kisses and got pink lipstick all over his face, but he didn't squirm around like a worm on a hook the way he usually did, he just smiled. I praised Vivienne for getting my brother to dress better, especially his present nicely baggy mauve silk shirt with a pattern of black chevrons.

"No one dresses me," Pete asserted. "I picked this out myself."

"Is that why you always used to wear the same two shirts before? White long underwear top with salsa stains and the other one that said NO TIME'S WASTED WHEN YOU'RE WASTED ALL THE TIME?" I laughed. "And those fatigue pants until they practically fell off your body?"

"Oh, I threw those out," Vivienne said. "Then Petey asked where are my clothes and I told him he didn't have any so he'd have to buy some more."

"I'll bet Petey loved that," I replied, and the two of them left still joined at the hip, Petey flipping me off at first but then turning it into a gracious wave at the very end. Madhu was leaving with her second sitting partner but stopped to ask about David as well.

"I'd was hoping he'd come in," she said. "He's one of my favorite attorneys at the firm. Never any attitude whatsoever. He seems quite genuine and interested in people."

"I think he is, yes," I agreed.

"It's a pity you broke off your engagement," she said. She was looking at me in a searching manner, and I wondered whether she was figuring the puzzle out. "We had a long talk about that, and other things."

"I think you should keep talking to him about things, if you don't mind," I urged gently.

She shifted her long twist of hair around to her other shoulder and nodded after a moment.

"Of course," she said. "I'll talk to David whenever he wants. Goodbye now."

And she was off with Geoff, the fake Earl Grey still leering like a creepy hyena at her and her new companion, until he turned round to me.

"Well, this was some show," he said. "Good spread, good turnout. By the way, you smell divine." He leaned inward while I recoiled. "What's the scent? I think I've smelled it before."

"You have. It's Abigail's perfume…Mitsouko," I answered.

"Oh, right…I like that idea," he winked. Like there was something titillating about us sharing perfume, like we had been spritzing each other with it on our naughty parts while getting dressed. "But you look familiar too, beyond the perfume." He scratched at his pointy chin. "Did we ever meet before? Maybe at a bar?" He laughed intimately while I kept myself from responding don't flatter yourself you skinny London wannabe.

"I don't believe so," I said, maintaining decorum. "I'm not much for hanging out in bars."

"I still say it's somewhere," he persisted. While we were talking I was clearing off tables, piling cups and saucers onto my wheel cart and scraping all the bread ends and lemon rinds into the trash; he watched keenly, and then he flipped his head back to get a better look and I remembered who he was. Before I had opened Samovar I had worked at a bunch of temp jobs while I saved enough money to start the venture, and he had been one of my assignments at a financial consulting firm. He had been a lazy sneaky shirker and had tried to blame me for messing up a report that he simply hadn't bothered to research. He had said I'd forgotten to add sections and then destroyed his data. Fortunately he had zero credibility among his peers so they had taken the word of a *temp* over one of their actual employees, but he had still accused me in front of a boardroom full of people and hadn't cared whether I'd lost my job.

I couldn't believe he wasn't connecting me to the incident, since I hadn't changed much since then in terms of age or hairstyles. He looked differ- ent—he'd lost some poundage and a moustache—but it clearly was him, even though I remembered his name as being Cliff. Cliff, Geoff, close enough. Still, in my case he probably remembered little since this had happened five years ago and he no doubt had many enemies among secretaries, temps, steward- esses, barmaids, and various other cast-off women, so he couldn't match a face to every one of us. Even though after I was through with the job I had anony- mously faxed a letter to him on the central office machine saying that my name was Gabriella Dolce e Gabbana from Rome and he, Mr. Geoffrey Hansen, had impregnated me despite the fact that he had a flabby little penis that kept fall- ing out. He had taken a trip to Italy the month before and kept bragging about all the hot pussy he'd gotten. And just to be sure that everyone had a chance to see it and he hadn't snatched it up himself, I had faxed the letter numerous times, at varying hours.

"Maybe we met in Italy…have you ever been there?" I said, trying not to laugh, but I also hurried to move my wheel cart back to the service area and whispered for Benny to hustle Fake Earl Grey out the door.

Benny hung around to help me finish cleaning and clearing—I think when you grow up in a restaurant family, wherever you are you always feel an obliga- tion to cook, serve or get leftovers off a table. While I bundled up tablecloths and napkins for the laundry he swept the floor and discussed the second tea partner he'd had.

"She was a registered, certified flirt," he assessed.

"Like you?" I asked.

"No, I'm a passionate amateur," he corrected. "I love women but I don't try to collect them. I honestly want to be with every single one that I flirt with. But with that woman, it's like a game to see how many guys she can hook. She puts you through the whole dance then tells you she has a serious boyfriend. A law- yer," he added, rolling his eyes. "Who'd ever want to marry one of them?"

"Oh, they're not all so bad," I said vaguely, then I picked up the last napkin and cursed that five-married broad for blotting her scarlet lips with it.

When we were through Benny asked if I wanted to go hang out at the Dan- gerous Toys' communal house in Logan Square but I took a rain check. He then handed me a package, a square padded envelope from my father. I took it and felt my heart balloon in and out; my father's handwriting was unusual and elegant, and he made European z's.

"I guess it's the picture of Grandma," he said, waiting while I opened it. My hands were shaking slightly; I expected a note but didn't see one, just the black and white photo of a dark-eyed young woman with some killer jewelry—jet pendant dangling earrings and a beaded choker. "Yeah, there she is," Benny confirmed, looking over my shoulder.

"Do you remember her?" I asked, studying the picture with a weird awe, like I was looking into a time warp mirror.

"Not too much," Benny said. "She died when I was about four. But I do remember that she made these cookies with powdered sugar and almonds, shaped like crescents, and she wore her hair in a bob like that photo, even though she was older. And I used to think she was a girl trapped inside a grandma's body because her eyes were so young and always laughing. I think I had a theory that if I cut her open while she was asleep the girl inside her would come out. I guess it's good that I never acted on that." He laughed. "Isn't it funny, though, what you remember even at that age?"

"It is," I agreed. "My mother's mother died when I was only six and I remember so much about her. She loved to drink Constant Comment tea, she smelled like Ponds Cold Cream, she wore a dressing gown with a fur-trimmed neck. She had been a model too, like my mother, only she'd modeled hats. She had a very long, elegant neck. Then she'd married my grandfather and settled down. They had a house in Oak Park with a porch swing and we'd hold our tea parties out there. She usually wore a charm bracelet with red and blue and purple stones. I can still see them picking up the sunlight when she poured the tea."

"Maybe your mind is like a brand new camera then," Benny suggested, pausing to sweep everything he had gathered into a pile right out the door. "Everything impacts it intensely and the lens is really powerful, but then when we get older we're distracted by other stuff and our own thoughts and the lens is dimmer." He glanced at the picture again and then back to me. "Nice. You do look like Grandma Fonseca. When she was in her prime."

"She's calmer," I observed. "But then she probably always knew who she was, where she'd come from, where she was going. Not like me."

"That could be because she was Portuguese," Benny said. "They're interesting people. Every time we visit I'm surprised at how they don't rush like Americans do, they don't push, they don't need to have everything right away. They talk to strangers in stores and smile on the streets. It's kind of refreshing. They seem to have a good thing going there, and they almost want to keep it quiet."

The CD player had cycled back to Gilberto and Gilberto, and Benny groaned. "I just said I like Portugal but I can't listen to this again, it's my day off. I'll check in with you later, all right? I'm going to split."

"Thanks, Benny," I said. "For the picture, for the tea, for the conversation. Tell Gilberto thank you too and stop by again when you're in town."

"Absolutely," Benny said. "Tchau."

"Tchau," I repeated, smiling and watching him go.

A few minutes later when I was sliding the photo back into the envelope, I felt something lodged at the bottom and pulled it out. Inside more bubble wrap was a tortoiseshell hair clamp with a folded note that read:

> **Before my mother cut her hair she used to wear it long like yours. This was among her things when she died and since my wife and daughter have short hair too, I thought you might be the best one to inherit it.**
>
> **By the way, my mother's name was Adelita.**
>
> **I hope that Benny has behaved himself and that you and I will see each other someday too.**
>
> **Affectionately,**
>
> **Your Father Gilberto**

Oh boy, I thought, get out your handkerchiefs, folks, this is a tearjerker moment…but I really didn't lose it, I just let out a big head to toe sigh, closed the blinds and took my own tea table, making a pot of Constant Comment like Nana Miller would fix while gathering up leftover cucumber olive sandwiches and the last peach caramel tart. I sat with Gilberto and Gilberto doing their thing, remembering Nana through the spicy orange rind taste of the Constant Comment and remembering Beth Miller through her *Splendiforous Camellia*, then taking in Adelita and her tranquil eyes. I put the comb in my hair and sat within the family vibe and began to think that maybe I knew where I was from and where I was going after all, even though it didn't seem so clear at times. Especially lately, but then wasn't that half the ride?

I was going to head home and take a shower since I had just gotten a glop of caramel sauce from the tart in my hair, but then I thought I should see Mike. I should show him that photo and the tortoiseshell comb now, not because I wanted to stroke his ego and make him feel like he was so important, but because in his own brash way he had forced me to meet my father and let me leave the encounter with more than a Fado matchbook. And because even Benny didn't know about the comb, it was just between me and my father and Mike would love to be part of that.

I turned off the lights and blew out the candles on the counter, then waited for Gilberto and Gilberto to finish. I had played the record so often that I knew it was the last song and that the final notes would drift away yet hang lightly in the air, like the perfume of a tea, like vapor, or like steam from a kettle of water just starting to really heat up.

0-595-31179-2